SNUFFED OUT

A Deadline Cozy Mystery - Book 2

SONIA PARIN

ISBN-10: 1537340778
ISBN-13: 978-1537340777

Chapter One
_____

"I'M dead on my feet. Honestly, whose idea was it to walk all the way into town? It doesn't feel so far when you're driving." Eve Lloyd flipped the menu over, and continued her search for a tantalizing treat. There had to be some sort of reward for her efforts, and she'd decided she needed to put some in.

She'd been baking up a storm for her aunt Mira, a.k.a. renowned historical romance author, Elizabeth Lloyd, who loved to nibble on a cookie or two while writing. And Eve liked nothing better than cooking for her. However, cooking and tasting went hand in hand and it was beginning to pile up on her.

There weren't any significant changes to her waistline... Yet. It had been a few months since she'd sold her restaurant and while her first attempt to relax had been sabotaged by a murder on the island, she'd eventually fallen in step with the slower rhythm of the small town. Hence her need for some extra physical activity...

A sugary treat, she knew, would defeat the purpose, but she wasn't willing to sacrifice all just yet. Besides, the long walk really had left her deflated and in need of an energy boost.

"Don't you have anything to say?" Eve asked. "What's the point of bringing you along if I'm going to talk to myself?" She set her menu down. "Jill?"

"Sorry, I got caught up in the collective silence."

"The what?" Eve looked around them. The Chin Wag Café was filled to capacity doing its usual mid-morning roaring trade. It was always as busy as a bee's hive with conversation buzzing...

Eve's eyes narrowed.

Everyone had fallen silent.

"What's going on?" She turned back to Jill who'd dipped her head behind the menu. "Jill?"

Grumbling lightly, Jill emerged from behind the menu and leaned forward. "Dead on your feet?" she whispered.

"Well, yes. Working as a chef, I've spent years on my feet. There's nothing wrong with my stamina, but honestly, I must have stepped on every single loose pebble along the way from Mira's house into town."

Jill's eyebrows curved upward. "Dead on your feet," she repeated.

"Okay. You're being blatantly obvious about something. What am I missing?"

Jill huffed out a breath. "The last time you talked about death, or murder or... killing... do I need to say more?"

Eve frowned. "Are you suggesting my choice of words had something to do with inviting a killer to the island?" It had been over two months since the unfortunate incident, which had resulted in the untimely death—

Her eyes connected with Jill's. Eve slumped back in her seat and glowered at her.

"What?" Jill asked.

"You've made me self-aware."

"Were you thinking about killing, death... murder?" Jill asked.

"You brought it up. My mind was on my sore feet and what I could eat to replenish my strength. The thought of having to trek back to Mira's on foot made me think this island needs a taxi service. But that was only a fleeting thought because now I'm thinking about..." she flapped her hands, "See what you've done? Now it's all I can think about." She scooped in a big breath. "All right. From now on, I will avoid all use of that word and all derivatives associated with it. Happy now?"

"You'll burst," Jill warned. "I give you an hour and I'm being generous."

"It's just a word."

"If you say so, but when it comes out of your mouth, it seems to gather momentum."

"You're being ridiculous and far too pedantic in your observations. You'll be the—" death of me, she finished silently.

"Yes?"

"I can do this. I can."

"Would you like to make it interesting?"

"A hundred dollars if I slip up," Eve suggested.

"A hundred? That's a bit steep."

"It shows how serious I am. I can go an hour without mentioning anything related to—"

"Yes?"

"You know very well what I'm referring to. And don't try to trip me up."

"Ready to order?" the waitress asked as she gave their table a brisk tidy up.

Eve hadn't seen her around before. She and Jill had become regulars at the café and Eve had made a point of being on first name terms with the staff. She looked at the girl's name tag.

Di.

Eve slanted her gaze toward Jill in time to see her friend trying to stifle her laughter.

She could do this. Eve gave herself a mental nudge and told herself to avoid all mention of that which she wouldn't even think about... or any words associated with it...

"I haven't decided yet," Eve said, "Perhaps you can help me. What can you recommend as a sure-fire pick me up decadent treat?"

"Death by Chocolate Fudge Tart," Di said.

Jill chuckled.

"Can we have another moment to decide, please?" Eve leaned forward and lowering her voice, said, "How far does this moratorium on anything associated with that which I won't mention because it'll cost me a hundred dollars go?"

"Don't mind me. Do and say as you please. I could do with an extra hundred dollars." Jill shrugged. "I'll have the blueberry pancakes and a double shot espresso, please."

Eve drew in a big breath and looked up at the waitress who'd already returned to take their orders. "I'll go with your recommendation and a double shot espresso too, please."

"Double shot espresso," Di wrote, "And...?"

"The tart you recommended."

"Which one?" Di asked, "I've just served two customers and they asked for recommendations too."

"I'd like the tart you recommended to me."

The waitress raised her shoulders.

Eve slanted her gaze at Jill who was pretending to be distracted by the pattern on the tablecloth. "Do you have the tarts listed on a board somewhere so I can point to the one I want? I don't see it anywhere on the menu."

"That's because it falls under the day's specials."

"Great, so you must have a specials' board."

"No, but I'll suggest it to the owner."

"Go ahead and order it," Jill said, her eyes sparkling with mischief.

Eve bit the edge of her lip. "May I?" She gestured to the waitress's order pad. "I'll write it down for you."

"If you can write it down, why not just tell me?" the waitress asked.

"It's the chocolate tart."

"We have several of those. Which one did you want?"

Eve threw her hands up in the air. "It's the Death by Chocolate Fudge Tart, all right. There, I said it."

"That was a quick hundred dollars. And I swear that was the sound of a second death knell," Jill murmured.

"Don't be so morbid. I'm going to change the subject and there'll be no more mention of... you know what." She drummed her fingers on the table trying to come up with something else to say.

She'd met Jill soon after arriving on the island to visit her aunt Mira who'd been away at the time, and they'd since become accustomed to each other's company. In fact, not a day went by when they didn't see each other or talk on the phone.

Jill was ten years younger than her but quite mature

for twenty-four. Something they had in common. At her age, Eve had been doing double shifts at a couple of restaurants trying to work her way up the ladder and get ahead in the competitive cutthroat world where men seemed to excel and get ahead far quicker than women.

"How's your painting going?" Eve rarely asked because she got to see her work-in-progress on a fairly regular basis as the house Jill shared with her parents' was only a short walk away from Mira's beach house.

"I'm thinking of tackling something bigger than the usual picture postcard size."

"I like small pictures," Eve said, "There's something intimate about the size. They can still make quite a statement. You know the Mona Lisa is ridiculously small. And then there's that Dutch artist... What's his name? He painted mostly small pictures. There was a film made based on a book written about him." She clicked her fingers. "Vermeer."

"Oh, yes. The Girl With the Pearl Earring."

Eve nodded. "Maybe I should open a gallery in town. Then I could display your work." She'd come to the island to spend some time redefining herself. The restaurant she'd owned with her then husband had suffered a near death—

Eve sprung upright in her chair and focused on navigating her way around any mention of death and killing and murder...

She gave a firm nod and tugged her train of thought

in another direction. She'd exhausted herself, revamping the business her ex had nearly sent bankrupt. She'd since sold it and had turned her back on the food industry. She hadn't exactly made a killing—

Eve pushed out a breath.

"What's wrong? Your face's gone all red," Jill said.

Eve fanned herself with the menu. "I'm thinking it's time I come up with a plan of action. I have some thinking time money, but I don't want to wait until my funds dwindle away."

"Why don't you work in Mira's bookstore?"

Eve had already considered that. Mira had purchased *Tinkerbelle's* Bookstore as an investment but the existing staff knew the business inside out. She'd have nothing to contribute. "I don't know anything about books."

"What's there to know?"

"What's hot, what's new." Eve lifted her shoulder. "You know I'm not a big reader."

Jill gave her a puzzled look. "There are days when I have to force myself to put a book down and get on with my painting, and that's something else I can't go a day without doing."

Eve played with the salt and pepper shakers. "Customers would expect me to know what I'm talking about. They'd want my expert opinion." Eve waved the idea away. "I'm not a complete philistine. I've made some headway with Mira's books. In fact, I just finished reading her latest manuscript." But only because Mira had said she wanted to base the swash-buckling hero on Detective Jack Bradford and Eve had been curious to see how he'd come across on the printed page.

She hadn't been disappointed.

"Are you experiencing some sort of early menopause?" Jill asked, "Your face flushed a deep shade of crimson again."

"Don't be ridiculous. Thirty-four year olds don't get hot flushes." Eve poured herself some water and drank deeply. "The more I think about it, the more curious I am about a gallery. I already like your paintings, so I shouldn't have any trouble promoting them."

"So you'll be comfortable if a customer makes a reference to Andrew Wyeth."

"Who's he?"

"One of my favorite artists. I have a poster of one of his paintings in my studio."

"Oh yes, he does those figures and landscapes. Very atmospheric... which is what you do in your landscapes."

"I'm impressed."

"Who else do you like?"

"Reginald Bryant Burns."

"He sounds stuffy."

"He's a recluse. Actually, he lives right here on the island."

Eve gave a pensive nod. "Now that I think about it, the name sounds familiar."

"He lives at the end of Old Coach Road."

"That's where the lighthouse is."

"That's the one. He bought it a few years ago."

"I used to hide out there when I was kid." Waiting for Frank Parkmore to go on one of his walks so she could sneak in and steal his roses to give to Mira. Eve fell silent and thought about Frank ending his days in a convalescing home after his stroke. Mira had visited him several times and had said his memory had gone. Just as well, Eve thought. It wouldn't be pleasant to think about the killer who'd been at large—

"I'd give anything to see his studio," Jill said.

"Hang on, I have heard of him." She tapped her chin trying to remember the details. "It was a newspaper article. Something about him making a killing—" Eve looked away. "How long does it take to make a cup of coffee and serve a piece of tart? I'm famished."

Jill laughed under her breath. "Those death knells are coming hard and fast."

Eve racked her brain trying to remember what she'd read. Something about him selling a drawing. "That's right. He sold a Picasso drawing. It was nothing but a scrap of paper and he got a mint for it. His grandfather had acquired it before Picasso had made a name for himself. Rumor has it, he has another drawing stashed away."

10

"He comes in here at about this time every day to get coffee right after he gets his donuts from next door."

They both looked up at the waitress.

"Sorry, I overheard you mentioning Reginald Bryant Burns."

"Thank you for the heads up." Eve turned to Jill. "This is exciting. Looks like you'll get your wish after all."

Jill shrunk back into her chair. "Wish?"

"You said you'd kill—"

"Yes?"

"You said you'd give anything to see his studio. When he comes in, we can ask him for a tour."

"So which part of recluse didn't you get?"

"He's an artist. He'll be delighted to show us around. Artists are full of themselves and always out to get attention."

Jill sighed. "He's one of the top guns in the art world, not a street artist peddling his wares. He's represented by one of the most prestigious art galleries in New York and has showings all over the world. The island is the one place where he can get away from it all, he said so in an interview."

Eve shook her head. "It would be a nice neighborly gesture. I bet he'll make an exception for us."

An hour and a half later, Eve caught the waitress's attention. "Another two coffees, please, Di."

Jill chuckled and rubbed her hands in glee. "Not for

me, thanks. I should go. Mischief and Mr. Magoo will be pacing by now. If they don't get their midday walk, they'll be restless in the afternoon."

"It won't kill you to wait another half hour—"

Jill laughed. "That's four hundred dollars you owe me."

Chapter Two

EVE STEPPED out of *Tinkerbelle's* Bookstore, her eyes pinned on the bakery across the road. She'd spent the last couple of days keeping a close vigil on the place, waiting for Reginald Bryant Burns to make an appearance.

Reggie boy wasn't making it easy.

If he didn't show up today...

Eve shook her head.

Reggie would show up. He had to.

Jill had said she'd love to have a tour of his studio and Eve had decided she would facilitate this.

Every time she saw Jill at her easel, Eve couldn't help being fascinated by the girl's passion. Painting hadn't been her first choice of career. In fact, Jill had stumbled on it as a therapeutic means of overcoming her dreadful experience in the high pressure world of fashion and magazines, her career there derailed by a dreadful boss.

Luckily for Jill, one door had closed and another one had flung wide open for her. While she picked up some cash doing occasional light cleaning for Mira, she made a decent living out of selling her paintings of seascapes to tourists.

Jill's enthusiasm had to be nurtured.

In her career as a chef, Eve had taken many trainees under her wing, thinking it was her duty to inspire them and guide them along their way.

She gave a firm nod.

Somehow, she would pave the way for Jill, with a view to eventually encouraging her to find a proper gallery to show her work.

First thing first, she thought.

From what she'd heard, Reggie liked his donuts and in regular doses. Had she already missed him?

She looked up and down the main street.

Every time a car pulled up she held her breath. That morning, she'd seen several new faces in town. There was nothing unusual in that. People drove in from the mainland to visit locals or to enjoy a day of walking along the many tracks crisscrossing the island. But today there seemed to be more new faces than usual.

She had no idea what he looked like.

The grainy photo she'd seen of him in a newspaper

had been too small to give her even a hint of his general appearance.

She meandered along the main street, stopping to read the new menu at Shelby's Table, one of the few restaurants on the island which stayed open all year round.

The Fall/Winter fare looked tantalizing. She'd been enjoying weekly dinners with Jack but had insisted on steering clear of the island, saying she preferred to stay under the radar and not become the subject of people's conversation. In case it didn't work out between them...

It had been two months of smooth sailing with the handsome detective she'd met recently... under unfortunate circumstances. She hadn't given any thought to where they'd be in twelve months, and she was in no hurry to tackle the subject. Her divorce had made her wary but not entirely cynical, she thought and turned her attention to the dessert list. Maybe, just maybe it was time to be seen out and about with Jack right here on the island as a show of faith that things would turn out well between them.

"Muddy Brownie Pudding with Honey Nougat ice-cream."

She'd have to walk twice around the island to burn that one off.

"Hey, there."

Jill!

"What are you up to, Eve?"

I'm killing time, she thought and swung around with a ready smile in place for Jill. "Dawdling. Hovering around. Shooting the breeze."

Jill's eyebrow lifted. "Looks to me like you're killing time."

"Quit taunting me. You've already cleaned me out."

Jill grinned. "No harm in trying. I've got my eye on a set of sable brushes but they're out of my price range."

"How did you get into town?" she asked when she didn't see Jill's bike secured to the bike rack.

"Samantha gave me a lift in."

"Since when are you two friends?"

"Since you encouraged me."

She had. Samantha was the same age as Jill and worked at *Tinkerbelle's* Bookstore, something else Jill could connect with, as she was a voracious reader.

Eve couldn't help feeling a twinge of envy with a tiny pinch of concern. Living on the island could be isolating and in the two months she'd been here, she hadn't made that many friends, not that she'd gone out of her way to meet new people.

"I suppose I'll have to learn to share you."

"Don't worry, there's plenty of me to go around." Jill smiled. "So what are you up?"

"I'm taking an interest in town activities. I'm always whizzing in and out and never stop to appreciate what goes on."

Jill studied her long and hard. "Out with it. What are you really up to?"

Eve looked over Jill's shoulder at a large black SUV that had just parked across the street and waited for the driver to emerge.

"I'm..." Eve narrowed her gaze.

"Eve."

"What?"

"Please tell me you're not waiting for Reginald Bryant Burns."

"What if I am?"

"You'll have a long wait. I hear he has house guests. He's not likely to leave them."

"Ha! That's how much you know. Look." She pointed at the man who was about to enter the bakery. "That has to be him. Come on."

"What makes you think—" Jill's cheeks reddened. "It is him. What are you going to do?"

She gave Jill's arm a tug. "Come and see."

When they strode into the bakery, Eve tried to reserve her opinions. Tried and failed. Reginald Bryant Burns was a mountain of a man, and as round as the donuts he was supposedly addicted to.

Jill jabbed her in the ribs. Don't, she mouthed.

Eve gave her a roll of her eyes and put herself directly in Reggie's path. "Excuse me."

Reginald Bryant Burns turned, his large meaty

fingers curled around a family sized bag of donuts, his beady eyes looking over her.

"Excuse me," Eve repeated. His gaze remained fixed on a point above her. Eve decided he was the type who didn't make eye contact with lesser beings. She lifted her chin up a notch. "I'm Eve Lloyd. And this is my friend, Jill Saunders. She's an artist too."

That got his attention.

When he finally looked down at her, Eve thought she caught him curling his upper lip at her. Again, she tried to reserve her opinions and instead searched for the slightest hint of friendliness.

"You're her favorite artist." She'd been saving the ego stroking remark as a backup, but his silence had unnerved her and the words shot out of her mouth before she could think better of it.

This time, he sent his gaze skating around Eve's face, his bushy eyebrows beetling down.

She waited for him to respond and when he didn't, she decided she needed to up her game and appeal to his benevolence. Everyone had some... "I'm trying to encourage her. I feel it's our duty to cultivate worthwhile interests in today's youth." She knew she was rambling but his silence now came across as annoyingly insensitive.

Just as she was about to dig deeper and step up her efforts again, he cleared his throat, his harrumph succinctly conveying a mixture of disapproval, impatience and indifference.

Eve wanted to believe she'd misread him, so she braced herself and surged ahead, this time scraping the bottom of her barrel for a final appeal. "You've been a huge influence to her and she greatly admires your work. If you saw her paintings you'd see how much talent she has. With the right guidance and encouragement—"

"Just what the world needs." His voice boomed and echoed around the bakery. "Another pretentious wannabe mediocre artist." He swept his massive hand across in front of her as if trying to swat her away.

Eve saw Jill shrink back. She didn't want to believe she was wholly responsible for the look of humiliation on her young friend's face. It seemed Reggie didn't care what people thought of him.

Telling herself to tone it down a notch, for Jill's sake, Eve smiled. "I realize this is an intrusion on your privacy, but if you knew how much Jill admires your work—"

He gave a loud huff. "Lady, I came in here to get my donuts. And not to listen to you babbling on about how much you appreciate my art."

Before she knew what was happening, he pushed and shuffled past her.

Eve lost her balance and backed into a trestle table stacked high with bags of chocolate chip cookies that went flying all over the floor. Trying to right herself, she slipped and fell on her butt.

A wave of gasps swept around the bakery.

"Clumsy as well as loud mouthed," he said and lumbered off, everyone in the store stepping back to clear the way for him.

Eve gasped.

As if to add insult to injury, the trestle table gave a final wobble, and collapsed and fell on her, the remainder of the bags sliding off and falling onto her prostrate body.

Eve's breath came hard and fast. "How... how dare you. You... you oversized egocentric... donut shaped selfish oaf. I never said I liked your art. In fact, I think it's overrated and will probably only be worth anything if someone does the world a favor and... and... and snuffs you out," she shouted after him.

Another gasp made the rounds of the bakery.

It took a few seconds for the bakery staff to respond and step forward to clear the mess.

"Are you all right?" Jill asked as she helped her up.

No, not really, but she would be. "My pride's been shattered. Otherwise, I'm fine. That odious man is so full of himself, he wouldn't need a life buoy to stay afloat." Eve sat up and raked her fingers through her hair, only then realizing everyone was hanging on her every word.

What had she just said? A jumble of words swam in

her mind. She'd called him an oaf and... Eve groaned. "I'm sorry, Jill. I ruined it for you."

"No, no you didn't," Jill said softly. "I wouldn't want to meet him now. He's horrible."

Eve couldn't bring herself to meet her friend's gaze. There was nothing worse than having one's dreams snuffed out.

"I promise, I'll make it up to you."

"Nonsense. Come on, let's go next door and have a coffee."

Chapter Three

"I THINK THAT'S EVERYTHING. Thank you for staying on, Eve. I always worry about leaving the house sitting empty while I go on one of my cruises."

Eve suspected this was her aunt's way of making her feel needed since the island had always been, at least until recently, crime free.

"My pleasure, Mira." As well as relief. This time, she knew where Mira was going and when she'd return. Eve shivered as she recalled arriving a couple of months before to an empty house and the chaos that had ensued... "I've packed some Macadamia and white chocolate brownies for the trip."

"Thank you." Mira smacked her lips. "What are you getting up to while I'm away?"

She'd be busy making amends. Mending fences.

Building bridges. She hadn't seen Jill in a couple of days and while Jill had assured her all was well, Eve had seen the signs of disappointment in her friend's face.

Eve wondered if she had all the necessary ingredients to make donuts. If she could rely on the old adage, she might find a way to Reggie's heart through his massive stomach.

"I'll find something to keep me out of trouble."

Mira gave her a warm smile. "Make that your operative word and you'll be fine."

Eve chuckled. "Have you been talking to Jack?"

Mira nodded. "It's refreshing to have a male point of view."

Eve smiled at her aunt's unexpected tact. So far, and to her surprise, Mira had avoided all mention of romance blooming between Eve and the local detective. "I see you've been using him to research another one of your books."

Mira smiled. "I've been playing around with the idea of branching out into suspense. I might even try my hand at weaving in a layer of fantasy."

"Please don't turn him into a werewolf. I'm not a big fan of fantasy books. I'll have nightmares about him."

"All right." Mira chuckled. "I think I have everything." Not one for drawn out farewells, she gave Eve a brisk wave, "I'll see you in a couple of weeks. Be good," and drove off, her mind probably already engaged in plotting her next novel.

Eve turned back toward the house, stopping for a moment to enjoy the view. If she stood there long enough, she knew the gentle lapping of the waves against the breakwater would lull her into complacency.

Relaxation was all well and good, however...

Soon she'd have to return to the real world, but first she had to find a clear trajectory, something to aim for and engage her interest.

She knew she could stay here for as long as it took to decide her next career move. In fact, if Mira had her way, Eve would make the island her permanent residence. But that wasn't something Eve was prepared to consider, not yet. A part of her still felt she needed to be 'out there', although, she wouldn't have any difficulty making the transition into island living permanent.

For as long as she could remember, the island had been her home away from home and Mira the mother she wished she'd had. She'd spent every summer vacation here, a cheerful highlight in her otherwise humdrum existence as a boarding school student.

Her relationship with her aunt had been easygoing, something her high achieving parents had always appreciated as it had minimized the disruption to their careers as high-flying lawyers. Eve had always known she'd been an accident but she'd adopted an air of pragmatism, making the best of the situation without kicking up a fuss, although there had been that one time she'd run away from school. At least they'd loved her enough to take care of her material needs until she could fend for herself.

She smiled and wondered if they would be as disappointed in her next career choice as they had been with her decision to become a chef.

While cooking would always remain an important part of her life, she didn't feel she had the passion to run a busy kitchen again. And after her encounter with Reginald Bryant Burns, the idea of owning a gallery had fizzled. She now knew she wouldn't have the patience to deal with delicate, overinflated egos.

She'd find something to do, eventually. She'd sublet her apartment in New York for six months. So she still had a decent chunk of time to play around with possibilities. And if worse came to worst...

She looked up at the house and then sent her gaze skating along the shoreline.

Jill had turned to the island as a refuge and appeared to be content with her life here. Perhaps not so much now that Eve had ruined her dream...

Eve sighed.

It had been a couple of days since she'd last seen Jill...

Eve decided not to read too much into it. For all she knew, Jill had thrown herself into one of her painting frenzies.

Sitting on the veranda, Eve's gaze bounced around all the knick-knacks and nautical ornaments Mira had collected throughout the years. There was a life buoy hanging by the window, some seashells glued onto the veranda post. A couple of interesting pieces of driftwood. She remembered seeing an old ship's steering wheel in one of the stores and made a mental note to buy it as her own personal contribution to the display.

She stretched her legs out and sighed. Thoughts of Jill returned. Eve had never seen her so crestfallen. She hated being responsible. If she hadn't felt compelled to interfere... If she hadn't been so pushy...

Eve nibbled the tip of her thumb. She'd meant well. Jill would have been inspired by a tour of Reginald's studio. It might have nudged her into doing something about increasing her reach. Selling her beautiful little paintings to tourists didn't compare to what she could achieve if she set her mind to working toward an exhibition at an art gallery.

The proper guidance by an established artist could launch her career.

Eve frowned. Had she even bothered to ask Jill how she felt about aspiring to greater heights?

When her cell phone rang, she let the call go to voice mail and sat there gazing out to sea for a while longer.

Half an hour later, she checked her message.

Abby Larkin.

Until recently, she'd owned *Tinkerbelle's* Bookstore. Now that she'd sold it to Mira, she was making a move to leave the island in search of her happy-ever-after.

"Please tell me you haven't left yet," she said when Abby picked up the call.

"Nope, still here but hoping to catch up with you before I do leave."

"Is dinner tonight too soon? I want to try Shelby's Table."

After they set up a time to meet, Eve checked the pantry and made a list of supplies to get the next day.

Unless she came up with a better solution, she'd be cooking up a storm to entice Reginald Bryant Burns into changing his mind.

She had single-handedly ruined Jill's chances of meeting him. It was now her responsibility to make amends.

"How final will your move be?" Eve asked Abby later that evening.

"I've put my house on the market..."

"We've only just met and now you're leaving to go in search of a husband..."

"Sorry, needs must..."

Eve took a sip of her wine, her gaze dancing around Shelby's Table.

This was her first visit to the restaurant, and definitely not her last. The homey atmosphere appealed on many levels, its rustic decor highlighted by a large fireplace with an old-fashioned stone hearth and a couple of comfortable looking leather chairs. A large cast iron candelabra hung in the center of the room, the candles casting a subtle light and adding to the intimate atmosphere. Antique looking oak tables and chairs were spread at roomy intervals. She could easily picture a romantic dinner for two.

On any day but today, she thought.

She tried to ignore the large group of diners congregated in the center of the room. Several tables had been joined to accommodate them. Their conversation came in waves, rising and falling. After polishing several bottles of wine, they were becoming quite boisterous.

Not surprisingly, the man commanding center stage in the lively group was none other than Reginald Bryant Burns.

Eve sent her gaze skating around the group of fifteen. His house guests, she presumed. A mix of men and women, both young and old, scruffy looking to impeccably stylish.

"You're not tempted to keep the house as a weekend retreat?" Eve asked.

Abby shook her head. "It would feel too much like a security blanket, here for me to come back to with my tail tucked between my legs. I need to make a clean break and stick to my purpose."

"Finding a husband who'll take you overseas on vacation?"

Abby grinned. "Yes."

"You seem to know what you want. You should have attracted someone, like a bee to honey. All these years owning the bookstore and not a single one of your customers caught your eye?"

"My customers are mostly women and anyone coming to the island for a getaway usually has a family in tow. He's out there somewhere, Eve, and I'm going to find him."

"Yes, you will." Despite her bitter divorce, Eve had refused to embrace a cynical outlook. Besides, Mira would never hear of it...

A burst of laughter echoed around the restaurant.

"... she gasped like a fish out of water. How... how... how dare you..."

Eve sprung upright in her chair.

Reggie was having fun at her expense, giving a blow-by-blow account of her pathetic efforts to engage his attention a few days before at the bakery.

His captive audience lapped it all up.

"And then she had the audacity to..."

Eve tipped her glass back, polishing off the rest of her wine in one gulp.

Unfortunately, Reggie had his massive back to her.

Otherwise, she would have speared him with a laser sharp glare.

"Oh, dear." Abby refilled her wine glass.

"I suppose you heard all about that."

"A whisper or two," Abby said, "It's strange. He's been coming to the island for a number of years now, and there's never been even a peep from him."

Eve laughed softly. "Suddenly I enter the picture and all hell breaks loose?"

"You weren't to know."

"What?"

"He's an artist and a recluse."

"Hardly. Look at him, playing host to all those ego stroking hangers-on." Even if she tried, she couldn't avoid hearing the rest of the conversation, or part of it, as the woman speaking hitched her voice.

"... That sounds like a threat. You might have just cause to pursue it..."

What? Abby mouthed.

Eve shrugged. She strained to hear more, but the group had huddled together lowering their voices. Just when it was all getting interesting, Eve thought. Her disappointment, however, was short-lived. Another voice piped in.

"... defamation... You have a reputation to uphold... Imagine if the newspapers get a hold of this."

Just great. He had a blood-sucking lawyer in his entourage.

"...Maybe that wouldn't be such a bad idea. We could do with extra publicity for your upcoming exhibition. The turnout last time was abysmal..."

Eve slanted her gaze toward the group and identified the person speaking. A woman dressed in casual elegance that spoke of ritzy trips to Paris for the Fall fashion shows. A gallery owner?

"You should take care, Reg. There might be others like her on the island. They could come after you with pitchforks. You're still an outsider here. What if they band together..."

Eve smiled. At least Reggie had one voice of reason in his group.

"Band together, and do what?" Reginald's voice boomed. "Ban me from town?"

"...It could happen. How would you feel about not being able to get your donuts or coffee?"

"Ha! I'd like to see them try. They need people like you and me here. Look around you. This place would be dead without us. It's not as if the cuisine here is anything to write home about..."

Eve smiled. She no longer felt quite so alone in her dislike of Reggie. That snide remark alone would be enough to get the restaurant owner and the chef on side.

Eve turned her focus back to her meal and tried to make the best of it. "I've been dying to try the dessert here but I don't want the experience ruined," she said and made a mental note to give Jill another hundred dollars. She set her knife and fork down in a huff. "I can't believe I was thinking of making him donuts as a peace offering."

"Arsenic laced donuts?" Abby asked.

"Arsenic would be too good for him."

Chapter Four

"GRAB THE BASKET. Put one foot forward. Now the
other. Good girl. Now... deep breath. On the count of
three, swallow your pride."

Eve's back teeth ground together. Despite what
she'd said to Abby the night before, she'd hit the ground
running that morning, rolling up her sleeves and baking
up a storm.

She could do this.

She didn't have a choice.

She had to do this.

Reaching the front door, she pinned her attention on
the door knocker shaped like a seahorse, drew in
another breath and knocked on the door, announcing her
won't-take-no-for-an-answer presence.

Worse case scenarios had been running through her

mind on a loop since she'd packed a basket full of donuts in her car and driven out to the lighthouse to do some serious groveling.

A slammed door in her face would barely pierce the surface of her thick skin. A snarl accompanied by a diatribe of snide remarks might manage to ruin her day, but overall, she felt confident in thinking no matter what Reginald Bryant Burns said to her, she'd shake it all off like the proverbial water off a duck's back.

If her courage dwindled and failed her...

No, her courage wouldn't dwindle because she'd stamped an image of Jill whooping with joy when she told her Reggie had changed his mind and had issued an open invitation for her to visit his studio.

She hadn't seen Jill for several days now, long enough for Eve to start thinking her young friend had decided she would be better off not knowing her.

A man with waves of hazel brown hair falling over one eye opened the door. His day old stubble enhanced his poster boy good looks. His easy smile gave Eve some much-needed courage.

"Hello, I come bearing gifts." She held the basket out.

"Do I know you?" he asked.

His sparkly blue gaze swept around her face and then did a thorough job of taking in every visible part of her body, and some not so visible, his eyes appearing to glaze over long enough for her to suspect him of trying to picture what lay beneath her clothes.

Either he was used to women enjoying his appreciative gaze or he didn't give two figs what people thought about him. Going by his looks, she'd say women clamored for his attention.

"I've seen you somewhere," he said.

"I doubt it. I'm only visiting the island." A half lie, she thought and wondered if she'd seen him out and about in town. She decided she hadn't, otherwise she would have remembered Poster Boy. Then again...

Had he been at last night's dinner?

Perhaps he'd had his back to her.

She wondered what he'd think if she asked him to turn around so she could have a look at his back...

"So what's this?" he asked.

"Donuts for Reginald Bryant Burns."

He chuckled under his breath. "I think I do know you. Or at least, know of you."

Eve shook her head. "I've been told I could work as a spy or secret agent because I look and sound average. No one would remember me."

"A nonentity?"

"Yes."

He folded his arms and gave a pensive shake of his head.

Eve took the opportunity to try and estimate his age. Mid to late twenties? He wore paint splattered faded jeans either as a statement or as a hazard of his occupation.

Just what the world needs...

Another artist.

"Whoever said you look average needs to have their eyesight tested. The bone structure of your face alone sets you apart from the average person."

Eve couldn't believe it. She felt a rush of heat sweep through her body and settle on her cheeks.

Jack complimented her. In fact, she'd seen him the week before and he'd told her she looked amazing. Granted, she'd worn a body hugging red dress and heels, making it practically impossible for him not to say something complimentary.

"Is there any chance of speaking with Reginald?" she asked.

Poster Boy gave her a brilliant smile. "I'm afraid not. Reggie hasn't come out of his studio all morning. He's in one of his painting frenzies. So these will come in handy. Save me the trip into town." He took the basket from her and gave the door a nudge.

"Oh, I see. Yes, of course. Well..." Before she could think of something useful or even intelligent to say, he closed the door.

Eve stood there, her mouth gaping open.

After much fuming over what could go wrong, on the drive over she'd turned her thoughts to a positive outcome. She'd been hoping to celebrate mission accomplished. Instead, well... she had no idea where she stood.

How much time would it take to bring Reggie to her way of thinking? Time... Nope, she hadn't taken that into account.

Or the fact it might take more than one batch of donuts to sweeten Reggie up, gluttonous oaf that he was.

―――――

Later that afternoon, Eve went back into town to while away some time. In reality, she wanted to increase her chances of encountering the sweet-toothed artist.

Not that she really thought that would happen any time soon. She'd seen Jill in one of her painting frenzies. The last one had lasted three days with very little sleep or food. With Jill's parents away on another one of their road trips, Eve had hovered around, cooking enticing tidbits just in case Jill got hungry. She'd also taken over dog walking duties. During the last couple of months, Mischief and Mr. Magoo had accepted her as an honorary member of their pack, happily trotting off with her.

Thinking it wouldn't pay to look too desperate or needy, she tried to make herself inconspicuous, forcing her attention into browsing mode. She visited one shop after another, taking her time, admiring the wares, and counting to ten before taking another step.

It nearly killed her.

She'd never had time to dawdle. Her daily schedules had always been packed to squeeze in as much as she could into her day, always keeping a cracking pace.

As for shopping...

It had never been her favorite activity. More often than not, she'd opted for online shopping.

After half an hour of browsing through The Mad Hatter's Tea Shop, she would swear she could list the entire contents without missing a single gimmicky teapot.

As she inspected the bottom of a teacup, the tail end of a conversation wafted her way.

"I didn't come all this way to go home empty-handed..."

Looking up, she didn't see anyone standing nearby. Eve leaned slightly and looked around the corner. There she saw a young couple.

They looked familiar. The girl, in her mid twenties, had long blonde hair cascading down to her waist and wore the latest in casual country wear, a cable knit sweater Eve knew must have cost a fortune, and fashionable skin-tight jodhpurs hugging her slim body, her riding boots screaming handmade. Her companion was roughly the same age, but with hair the color of dark chocolate. He had the sort of preppy look Eve had become suspicious of because it spoke of entitlement, but mostly because it reminded her of her ex husband.

Setting the teacup down, she continued her pretense of browsing, and tried to move within easier earshot of the conversation, which was about to get heated, Eve thought watching the girl jab a finger against the young man's chest.

"You said this would be a cinch," the girl said.

"Mel—"

"Don't you Mel me."

"You said you knew how to play him—"

"I'm out of here," the girl huffed out. "Do it before the week is out. I can't waste another week of my life waiting for you to grow a backbone..."

The couple left the store still arguing.

Eve tried to remember if they'd been part of Reggie's entourage. She'd only really noticed the woman she'd assumed was a gallery owner. There had been five women. The girl, Mel, could possibly have been among them. Why couldn't she remember?

As she turned, her gaze met the store clerk. A blonde girl...

Blonde...

The women at the restaurant had all been blonde.

She looked out the store window at the street opposite. The bakery door swung open and Jill stepped out.

Eve wished she had good news for her.

She considered inviting her to dinner but common

sense told her to give Jill more time to cool off. She hadn't said anything, but Eve knew she couldn't possibly be happy about recent events.

She turned back to pretending to admire the teapots on display.

"You are not seriously thinking about taking up tea drinking."

Relief swept through Eve. "Why not?" She turned and smiled at Jill who'd come into the store.

"Your body would go into meltdown, the earth would tilt on its axis, disrupting the orbit of the moon and in turn, playing havoc with the tides."

"I don't drink that much coffee."

"I've never seen you drink anything but coffee." Jill gave her a small smile. "I saw you coming in and after twenty minutes decided you needed rescuing."

"You know me too well." Eve realized Jill knew she'd been up to no good. The knowing smile said it all, but Jill didn't reprimand her for still trying to catch sight of Reginald. "Mira's gone off on her cruise." Eve felt her cheeks redden. "I don't suppose you'd like to have dinner with me?"

"Are you cooking?"

Eve nodded and bit off the sudden urge to tell Jill she'd missed her these last couple of days. "We could make a night of it," she said and hoped she didn't come across as too needy.

"That would be good. My folks are planning their

next road trip and bickering about whose turn it is to choose the destination. I'm trying to stay out of their way because they seem intent on dragging me along too."

"How does tomorrow night sound?"

"Perfect."

"I assume you've just had a coffee. At the risk of coming across as too clingy, is there any chance you might have room for another?"

"Coffee and cake," Jill agreed.

With Mira gone on her cruise, it took Eve a couple of hours to get used to being alone in the house again. After having a bite to eat, she strode out to the beach and walked along the shore for a bit. The sky provided a blanket of twinkling stars for her to gaze at. In the distance, she watched a yacht disappearing into the horizon and heard seagulls squabbling over a tasty find.

If she stayed on in the island, she decided she would have to seriously consider adopting a dog she could take out for walks.

Time to start a pros and cons list, she thought and mentally divided a page into reasons why she should stay on and reasons why she should return to New York.

With enough moonlight to navigate by, she continued her walk, every now and then crouching down to pick up a seashell. Along the way, she stopped to inspect a piece of driftwood. The trunk had some lovely twists and interesting gnarls. She tried to lift it but it was too heavy. Looking back at the house, she calculated the distance she'd have to drag it.

Putting some more effort into it, she managed to dislodge it but didn't get very far.

"A rope would do the trick."

Sprinting back to the house, she hunted down an old rope from the front veranda. The brilliant idea as well as her intention to haul the piece of driftwood back to the house weren't enough. She still needed to put some brawn into the task.

With the rope tied securely around the trunk, she dragged it half way back and had to stop to catch her breath and give her hands a rest.

"Heave-ho, Eve. You can do it." Her arms ached from the exertion and the rope chafed her hands, but she'd already committed to the task.

It took her several goes to get the trunk to the house. By then, she'd had to dangle a carrot as a reward in the form of a tall glass of wine or two. When she reached the front veranda, her hands shook, but nothing beat the sense of satisfaction she got from seeing the lovely piece alongside the rest of the nautical paraphernalia.

Back inside the house, she put on some music, cleaned the kitchen and, to her surprise, spent the rest of the evening reading a book, choosing one from Mira's favorite collection of fantasy romances.

While she managed to get through a quarter of the novel, it didn't surprise her when she woke up in the sitting room where she'd fallen asleep.

"Eve, better take yourself off to bed."

Yes, she'd definitely get a dog.

"That way, I won't have to be so obvious about talking to myself."

As she made her way toward the stairs, she saw the phone message light blinking, but decided to leave it until the morning.

If anything had happened to Mira, the call would come through to her cell phone, so just to be on the safe side, she checked it. Nothing. Meaning she had no urgent need to check the message.

She set her book down on the bedside table thinking she would finish it the next night, and went to draw the curtains close.

Looking out the window she noticed the sky had clouded over. Eve smiled. She'd been lucky to enjoy the display of sparkling stars before the weather changed.

As she was about to draw the curtains, something caught her attention.

The lighthouse.

She couldn't remember the last time she'd seen it working, yet there it was, the intermittent light blinking, almost as if trying to taunt her with a reminder of the oaf who lived there.

Belatedly, Eve realized her offering of donuts had been a bad idea. It would be an entirely different story if she could somehow cut off his supply from the bakery.

Then, she'd have him eating right out of her hand...

Chapter Five

THE NEXT MORNING, Eve had to use every inducement under the sun to get herself out of bed. Hauling the
piece of driftwood the night before had left her
exhausted. Her arms ached and her hands felt slightly
swollen.

She had a dinner to plan for Jill. It would go some
way toward mending the rift between them. Jill would
deny its existence, but Eve knew she'd put her foot in it.
She owed her friend big time.

A long shower, with the water gushing out as hot as
she could take it without suffering third degree burns,
went a long way toward soothing her aching muscles.
The strong cup of coffee she made finished the job,
giving her a much-needed boost in energy and
enthusiasm.

She grabbed her shopping list and rushed out of the house only to double back when she remembered the message she hadn't listened to the night before.

She hadn't missed one message. She'd actually missed two.

"You baked donuts for that oafish man?"

How had Abby found out?

The second message came on.

"Word is you tried to poison Reginald Bryant Burns. Call me."

Poison?

Eve drove into town at breakneck speed and made a beeline for the travel agent's office. Helena Flanders greeted her with a gurgle of laughter.

"I had the most entertaining night eating at The Galley Kitchen."

"Don't tell me, Reggie was there with his hangers-on."

Helena clapped her hands. "They were hanging on his every word. He said he'd had to make an appearance in town to show everyone he wasn't intimidated by you."

"Me?"

"Apparently, your donuts gave him the runs. He said his strong constitution saved him from a bout of food poisoning."

Her lips moved but no sound came out.

"If you're thinking of setting up another restaurant here on the island, I'd wait for the furor to die down. It's all anyone can talk about this morning."

"M-my donuts... my donuts gave him the runs?" she finally managed to say.

"What on earth possessed you to bake them for him? I heard about your run-in with him at the bakery."

Again she tried to speak, but her words got all clogged up in her throat. She'd kill him.

Helena patted her shoulder. "He's clearly baiting you."

"Why?"

"The man has a humongous ego. I hear things are not going well for him. He hasn't sold a single painting in over a year. You've become an easy target for him."

"He's taking his frustration out on me?"

"That's what bullies do, dear. I'm afraid you picked on the wrong man."

"But... but... I didn't pick on him. I just wanted him to invite Jill to his studio."

"Yes, and when that failed you tried to poison him."

"Don't be ridiculous."

"Well, that's what he's going around saying. Come on, I'll buy you a coffee. This will all blow over. He only stays here for a month or so."

Eve returned home with her purchases for the dinner she'd promised Jill. After her coffee with Helena, she'd dropped in on Abby who'd been busy packing up for her trip.

She too had been out eating at The Galley Kitchen the night before. Rather than being amused, she'd been as furious as Eve had been over Reginald's behavior.

He'd again been entertaining his full entourage, something Abby had found disheartening saying that if the ten men in the group were representative of the wider population of men, she didn't stand a chance of meeting her perfect match.

While they'd tried changing the subject several times, they'd kept coming back to Reginald's accusations.

Setting her grocery purchases down on the kitchen counter, Eve decided she needed to go out for a long walk to blow off some steam or she'd end up serving Jill a plate full of her anger.

She walked along the well-trodden path running alongside the shoreline, occasionally meandering onto the beach and then back to the path.

With no particular destination in mind, she lost track of time and only turned back when she began feeling slightly better.

Back at the beach house she was surprised to find Jill had already arrived and was waiting for her on the veranda.

"Did I get the date wrong?" Jill called out.

Eve trotted up the steps. "No, I just need to get myself a watch. Come on in, you can keep me company while I cook."

"Where did you get to?"

"Nowhere... out for a walk. I needed to take care of something." To eject all the thoughts that had been plaguing her. "Come on, I'm starving and I'm making your favorite dish."

"Anything you cook is my favorite. Lead the way."

In the kitchen, Eve dug around the refrigerator and brought out a chicken."

"Oh," Jill said.

"Oh?"

"We're having chicken. I thought you said you were cooking my... Never mind."

"But you like chicken."

Jill shrugged and turned away. "Has Mira done something with the decor?"

Eve sighed. "It just clicked. Extra large pizza with the lot. That's your favorite." Eve raised her hands palms up. "Sorry, they're not up to kneading dough."

"What happened?"

"Oh, nothing." She selected a bottle from one of the many she'd purchased that day and poured them each some wine.

"Um... hitting the bottle?" Jill asked.

"I thought we'd make it a proper girls' night in and let our hair down. You should stay the night."

"You won't need to ask me twice. My parents ganged up on me today. They're saying I'm at risk of turning into a hermit and should go with them on their next road trip. They're trying to sweeten the deal by including a stopover in Washington. They even compiled a list of museums for me to visit."

"Don't they know all the worthwhile galleries are in New York?"

Jill laughed. "Can you picture us driving up Fifth Avenue in our Winnebago? Oh look, honey, that there is Central Park. Can we go around it again? A park, where, where? Not a park, honey, Central Park. Laura, please, I'm trying to find a place to park," Jill said mimicking her parents.

Eve laughed. "We should plan a trip to New York. Or maybe you can come visit me."

"So you've decided, you're leaving."

"What?" Her heart gave a sudden thump, "No. It's all still up in the air." Eve swung away and pressed her hand to her chest. If her overreaction was anything to go by... Was it? Was a part of her ready to dig her heels in? Was she that divided about leaving... or staying?

"I'm thinking of getting a dog," Eve said.

"Quick change of subject, but I'm willing to go with it. What type of dog?"

"A companion. A friendly dog."

"I meant, what breed?"

"Oh... I haven't given that any thought. Your Labradors are placid. But I'll probably end up getting something smaller." She shrugged. "Something that'll only want short walks." She prepared a cheese platter and some bread. "Come on, let's go nibble on these and drink lots of wine while the chicken cooks."

She collapsed on the couch and took a long swig of her wine.

"Looks like you needed that."

"You've no idea." She wished she could decompress and tell Jill about her day, but that meant talking about Reggie and Eve felt it had become a sore point of contention with them. Jill had most likely heard about Reginald Bryant Burns' latest verbal assault on Eve but she hadn't mentioned it, so Eve decided to leave it alone. Besides, it had taken her a long walk to shake it all off and she didn't want to wind herself up again.

An hour later they'd settled down to dinner, a second bottle of wine and a lengthy discussion about pets.

With enough wine in her system, Eve forgot to avoid all mention of Reggie.

"Is Reginald Bryant Burns married?" she asked.

"Divorced, several times," Jill said. "What's for dessert?"

"Ice-cream. Sorry, I didn't have time to bake."

Jill gave her a slanted eye look.

"What?"

"Do you have any idea how odd that sounded coming out of your mouth? You always have time to bake. We could be about to face a tsunami, and you'd still manage to throw some ingredients together and cook something for the ride."

"I'll make it up to you, I promise. It's just been one of those days." She couldn't help wondering if any of the women present at dinner the other night had been Reggie's ex-wives. "What about children?"

"What about them?"

"Does he have any?"

"Oh... him. No. None. Why do you ask?"

"He and his group were having dinner at Shelby's Table the other night and I was just wondering about the people who'd willingly spend time with him." Then again, she'd been referring to them as hangers-on. Those types, she thought, had to have ulterior motives for being with him. Perhaps some were trying to gain a share of the spotlight. A young artist would definitely benefit from the association.

"How about a Beagle?" Jill suggested.

It took Eve a moment to remember they'd been talking about pets. "I hear they're not very loyal."

"You want exclusive rights?"

Eve shrugged. "I'd like a pet who'll listen to me when I call him."

"He'll probably listen but he might not respond."

"Well, I want one who'll respond."

"You have to train them to do that."

"I hadn't thought about it."

"Haven't you ever owned a pet?" Jill asked.

Eve shook her head. "We weren't allowed to have them at boarding school." Eve finished her wine and got up. "Rum Raisin Chocolate ice-cream?"

"Yes, please."

She prepared two bowls filled to capacity, added a sprinkle of walnuts and set them on a tray with another bottle of wine and fresh glasses.

"Ice-cream and wine?" Jill asked.

"It can't hurt."

"I'll ask again tomorrow." Jill stretched out on the couch and dug into her ice-cream. "I heard Reginald had another altercation at the bakery."

"When?"

"Yesterday. He went in to complain about the donuts. Said they'd given him the runs."

"Oh." Eve sat up and topped up their glasses. She didn't want Jill to know she'd gone to the trouble of baking the man a batch of donuts and she still couldn't believe they'd made him sick.

Her donuts.

They had to have been the ones from the bakery.

He'd eaten two lots?

The man gave gluttony a bad name.

"They banned him."

Eve's mouth gaped open. "I should be careful what I wish for." She had him right where she wanted him. If she waited a couple of days, she could then approach him again, never mind that he'd launched a serious smear campaign against her donuts. He'd be desperate for them... salivating... drooling. Begging her for them.

"Do you think he'll go into withdrawal?" Jill asked.

She was counting on it.

Eve sat forward and looking out the window, she narrowed her gaze. "Did you see that?"

"I saw something," Jill said, "What was it?"

"It might have been a balloon," Eve said.

"I don't think so. Look, there it is again. Now it's gone." Jill surged to her feet and strode toward the French doors. "It's round. There it is again."

"Yes, but what is it?"

"It makes me think of the bat signal."

"A donut signal?" Eve's mouth gaped open. "It really does look like a donut." A giant donut reflected against the clouds.

"Why does it keep appearing and disappearing?"

They both stepped outside and looked toward the end of the cove.

"The lighthouse. The light's on again. Do you think it's coming from there?"

Jill giggled. "Maybe Reggie's sending out a signal for more donuts."

They stood there watching it until they both started to shiver from the night air and went back inside to polish off the rest of the wine. By the end of the third bottle, they'd forgotten all about the lighthouse.

Chapter Six

_____

"I RESERVE the right to say I told you so."

Eve sunk down in the passenger seat of her car and blinked. "FYI, I just blinked in agreement." Eve winced, the sound of her own voice too loud for comfort. "Tell me again why we couldn't have breakfast at the house."

"You need a breath of fresh air well away from the smell of wine still lingering in the house."

"So why are you so bright-eyed and bushy-tailed this morning?"

Jill shrugged. "I'm young."

"What does that make me?" Eve grumbled under her breath. "And what's with breaking the speed limit?"

Jill shifted in her seat. "I... I just want to beat the morning rush hour."

"We're the only ones on the road," Eve said.

"The rush hour at the café," Jill said as they drove past it.

When Jill reached the end of the street and appeared to be aiming the car toward a space, Eve cringed. "Do me a favor and drop me off outside the café."

"But that means driving around the block again."

"And your point is?" Eve asked.

"What happened to your health kick?"

Eve shrugged. "Nothing but a fad."

Jill pulled up outside the Chin Wag Café and, glancing out the driver's window, peered up and down the street.

"Are you looking for someone?" Eve asked.

"No."

"Is there someone you want me to keep an eye out for?" she asked and bobbed her eyebrows up and down.

"It's amazing how cunning you can be even with half your brain cells shuffling around with a hangover."

"Practice makes perfect. Now go park the car. I'll get us a table." Eve slid out of the car and focused on taking one step at a time as she wondered if someone had caught Jill's attention. Living on the island meant her choices were limited. The island wasn't exactly a magnet for young men her age...

"Hey, there."

Turning required far too much effort so she waited for the person who'd spoken to approach her.

"See, I recognized you."

Poster Boy!

She remembered babbling on about being a nonentity and not having a memorable face the day when she'd taken the donuts over to the lighthouse... "Hello, what brings you to town?"

He raked his fingers through his hair. The poor boy looked frazzled. Pushing out a breath, he pointed at the bakery.

"Doing a donut run?" she asked as the previous night's conversation swum in her head. Reggie boy. Banned from the bakery. Ha! Of course, he'd send someone in to get his fix.

Poster Boy waved a piece of paper. "My to-do list for the day. Get Reggie his donuts." He shoved the paper inside his pocket and shrugged. "I tried to get some, but word has spread. We've all been banned from the bakery."

"We?" She supposed he meant the entire entourage.

He grinned. "I don't suppose..."

Eve folded her arms across her chest. "You don't suppose what?"

He brushed his hand across his face.

Eve leaned forward. "You've got a smudge."

"A what?"

"A smudge on your cheek."

He swiped his hand over it and only managed to make it worse.

"Still there."

He brushed his other hand over it.

"It's gone now."

"I have a proposition for you," he said, "How about I buy you a cup of coffee. You look in need of one."

"Lead the way." Inside the Chin Wag Café, Eve forced herself to crank up her brain. She needed to be tactical and not come across as too desperate. Realizing she held the upper hand, she decided she had to play it to her best advantage. "It seems I have something you want."

He gave her a boyish grin. "And you want to negotiate."

They sat at a table by the window. Seeing Jill approaching, Eve knew she needed to work fast. "Okay, let's put our cards on the table. You want donuts and I want to get access to Reggie's studio."

He took a second to think about it and then nodded. "How soon can you deliver them?"

Eve scooped in a big breath and geared herself up. "What's the best time for my friend to visit the studio?"

Poster Boy brushed his hand across his chin. "How about Friday week."

"No studio visit. No donuts."

"You don't trust me?"

"Do I look as if I trust you?"

He sighed. "Okay. When do you want to do it?"

"Today."

"Today?" He shook his head. "I don't know if I can swing that."

Seeing Jill about to enter the café, she said, "You have ten seconds to decide. It's your choice."

"You're twisting my arm. All right. How long does it take you to bake them?"

"Two hours. I can be there by midday." That would be long enough for her to consume copious amounts of coffee and then get some donuts from next door. There was no way she'd be baking a fresh batch.

"You drive a hard bargain. Okay. I'll see you then." He got up and left.

A second later, Jill sat down, her cheeks glowing bright pink, her gaze following Poster Boy as he crossed the street.

"Even in my morning after haze I can recognize the spark of interest," Eve said.

"What?" Jill asked.

"I knew there had to be a reason for you to be in such a hurry to get to the café."

"I don't know what you're talking about."

"You've got your eyes on Poster Boy." Eve grinned. She was going to kill two birds with one... bag of donuts.

"I suppose ours is not to reason why," Jill said under her breath.

"Speak up, I think I'm losing my hearing."

"Nothing." Jill huffed. "Okay, why did you buy an extra large family size bag of donuts? It doesn't make sense."

"Is it meant to?"

"Shouldn't you be having a hair of the dog—"

"Ugh! Wine? This early in the morning?"

"It's nearly midday. Is your hangover still lingering?"

Grumbling, Eve set the bag of donuts she'd just purchased from the bakery in the back seat and then buckled up for the ride home.

"I guess I'm driving again. Now, are you going to tell me why you needed so many donuts?" Jill asked.

"It's a surprise."

"I don't like those," Jill said, "They can blow up in your face."

"I suppose you'll put two and two together soon enough." And if Jill really did have her eye on Poster Boy, she might appreciate a moment or two to brush a comb through her hair. "We're delivering these to the lighthouse."

"What?" Jill slammed her foot on the break.

"I've cut a deal with Poster Boy. In exchange for the donuts, he'll get us into Reggie's studio. We'll go in, have a look around, you can ask Reggie questions, but don't expect him to answer."

"What about all the stuff Reginald Bryant Burns has been saying about you?"

"All forgotten... for the greater good."

"You have no pride."

"Pride doesn't serve any purpose in life other than to hold you back. Now drive. I need a proper breakfast and there's some bacon and eggs with my name on them at home."

"Do you think the others will be there?" Jill asked as they made their way to the lighthouse.

"Who?"

"The wives. The gallery owner... and the others. I've seen them around town."

"Are you saying those elegant looking women were married to him? What could have attracted them to a man like him? Not his charm..."

"There's no accounting for taste. You know the artist Frida Kahlo was madly in love with the Mexican muralist, Diego Rivera. And he was... robust."

Eve slanted her gaze at Jill. She'd assumed Jill had been keeping an eye out for Poster Boy. But what if... "Um... Jill?"

"Yes?"

"Just how fond are you of Reggie's art?"

"I'd happily clear out all the pictures hanging on my walls to make way for one of his paintings."

"What about the man?"

"Oh... I'm willing to make concessions."

"You are? You don't think he's... a bit too old for you?"

"Who?"

"Reggie."

"Ugh."

Eve sighed her relief. "For a moment there I thought I was going to have to hit the bottle again."

"You thought... Me and him? What gave you that idea?"

"Well, in a strange way, it sort of made sense. You love his art, I imagine loving the man would be the natural next step."

"Promise me you'll never try to imagine me with a man who's old enough to be my father. It's icky."

"Okay."

Jill looked over her shoulder at the back seat. "One more question. Why did you put the donuts in a basket?"

"Presentation," Eve said and looked out the passenger window.

"I doubt he'll notice or appreciate the gesture."

Reggie wouldn't. But she'd promised Brandon she'd bake the donuts herself... not that it would have made

SONIA PARIN

any difference. Although, now that she thought about it, Brandon had looked quite relieved when she'd said she'd bake them. Did that mean Reggie preferred her donuts over the bakery's?

Just as they were pulling up to the lighthouse, Eve's cell phone rang.

Jack!

"Hello there, stranger. Have you emerged from your backlog of paperwork unscathed?" She imagined him brushing his hand across his face.

"All done," he said. "Did Mira meet her deadline?"

"Yes, her latest manuscript is now in the hands of her editor." She felt a light blush rise up to her cheeks as she thought about Jack being the inspiration for Mira's swashbuckling hero.

"Eve."

The sound of her name on his lips made her smile. "Yes."

"Are you staying out of trouble?"

She sat up. "Yes, sir. I am."

"Are you sure?"

She had to wonder if Jack had a sixth sense. "Absolutely sure."

"You hesitated."

"Jill's driving and I need to keep my eye on the road. You know what they say about two heads being better than one." Eve could easily imagine Jack smiling.

"Now you sound as if you're trying to cover your tracks."

"And you sound like a detective."

He chuckled lightly. "Friday night is looking good for me. How about you? Are you free?"

"Absolutely." She glanced over at Jill who did a good job of pretending she wasn't listening to the conversation. "I've tried out Shelby's Table in town. The food is superb."

"Dinner on the island?" he asked, his voice carrying his surprise.

Until now, she'd insisted on meeting him on his home turf on the mainland. Eve gave a small nod. Yes, it was time to step it up. Eve took a moment to check how she felt about it. "Yes. Dinner on the island."

A moment of silence followed. She wondered if Jack had sat back to think what it might all mean. Eve bit the edge of her lip. What if he'd been comfortable with the way everything had been moving? Slowly.

"I'll pick you up at seven."

She closed her eyes and smiled. Had she remembered to add Jack to her pros and cons list? His name would definitely tip everything in favor of staying on in the island.

After disconnecting the call, Eve hugged the phone and enjoyed the buzz of excitement surging through her.

"Okay. We're here. How does my hair look?" Jill asked.

Eve had never seen Jill looking so jittery. "Your hair looks shiny and in place."

"Do you think he'll mind if I take some photos?"

"He'll probably be too busy stuffing himself to care." She hauled the basket from the back seat and followed Jill who'd trotted ahead of her like a kid eager to get to the candy store.

The door opened immediately after they knocked and Poster Boy took the basket and waved them in without saying a word.

Eve looked at Jill and shrugged.

Inside, the place was as quiet as a cathedral.

"Where is everyone?" Eve asked.

"Gone to lunch in town."

"Um... sorry, I didn't catch your name."

"Brandon. Brandon McKay."

He led them along a narrow corridor and through a door that opened to a large, high-ceilinged room.

The studio. At the end of one wall stood a large easel with a huge canvas on it and a stuffy old chair in front. Trestle tables lined the walls, some with stacks of paper, others with mounds of paint tubes and brushes and a selection of bottles. Varnish. Turpentine. Painting medium...

"What's that dreadful smell? Eve asked and covered her nose. "It's so pungent."

"Turpentine," Jill said and rushed toward the canvas where she stood staring at it with her mouth gaping open. It was massive and covered with large blocks of faint washes. A work in progress, Eve assumed.

"So... is the man around?" Eve asked.

Brandon shook his head. "No. I'm afraid I couldn't swing that."

Jill didn't seem to mind. She stood there absorbed in the painting. After a few moments, she pulled out her camera and began taking pictures.

Eve tried to find something to like about the painting, but it seemed too... too faded, too vague, as if the artist couldn't quite grab hold of an idea.

"So... are you some sort of groupie?" she asked Brandon.

"Reggie's mentoring me."

"You're an artist."

"I'm working toward my first show."

"Where's your stuff?"

"Stuff?" he asked and edged toward the door.

"Your work. Your paintings."

"Back at my studio in the city."

"Taking time out, are you?" Eve asked as a way of buying Jill more time in the studio.

He frowned. "I'm working on some drawings."

"Are they like blueprints?"

He nodded and took another step back toward the door. Eve could swear he was about to break into a sweat.

She sidled up to Jill. "You look as if you're having a religious experience," she whispered.

"Trying to," Jill said.

Behind them, Brandon shuffled his feet. "Um..."

"Ready?" she asked Jill.

"Yeah, I guess."

Eve gave Brandon a small smile. "Pity we missed the man himself. You'll be sure to tell him we came by," she couldn't help teasing.

He stepped aside to let them through.

Eve stopped and turned back. "By the way, I saw the lighthouse light on the other night and last night again." She wasn't sure, but she thought Brandon flinched. "It hasn't been working in a while. I was surprised."

He shoved his hands inside his pockets. "Reggie likes to tinker around. I guess he fixed it."

Reggie, a Mr. Fixit Man? She couldn't imagine it.

"Thanks for the tour, Brandon."

He nodded. "See you around town."

They made their way to the car, neither one saying anything until they were half way home.

Jill cleared her throat. "That was hardly worth our time. But thank you for organizing it."

Eve tapped her chin. Brandon hadn't said anything about organizing more donuts. She wondered if that meant their stay on the island was coming to a close. "You didn't like what you saw?"

"I expected more. His paintings are usually so

simple... yet complex. Maybe it wasn't finished."

Or maybe, Reggie was finished.

Eve remembered Helena's remark about him not selling anything in a while...

"Perhaps he's missing a muse. Hey, maybe that's why his ex-wives are here. You know, spark off the old magic again."

Jill shook her head. "There was something odd about that painting. I can't put my finger on it."

"Are you up for some lunch? I'm buying. Maybe some food will help you think."

"Sure," Jill said, in an absent tone that suggested she was still immersed in the painting.

Eve pulled out her cell and did a quick search for the gallery representing Reginald Bryant Burns.

A website came up.

The gallery represented several artists and had a page for each one. She scrolled through to find a display of Reggie's art.

Expensive, Eve thought.

She kept scrolling and came across some smaller works within her price range. A few minutes later, she sat there gazing at one that had caught her eye. It would cover Jill's wall very nicely.

She emailed an expression of interest, made a deposit and mentally worked out when it would be convenient for her to drive in to the city to finalize the sale.

Chapter Seven

EVE GRABBED a bottle of wine and a couple of glasses and took them into the sitting room. "You've been very pensive and doing a thorough job of blending in with the couch. What's going on, Jill? Are you still disappointed we didn't catch sight of Reggie at lunch?" After dropping off the donuts at the lighthouse, they'd driven into town to have lunch and had walked the length of the main street looking for the artistic entourage, but they'd been nowhere to be found. Then Di, from The Chin Wag Café, had mentioned they'd ordered a picnic lunch and had gone trekking to the far end of the island.

"I'm thinking about my little paintings," Jill said.

"Size doesn't matter," Eve assured her.

"Yeah, right. How am I ever going to become a serious artist if I can't fill up more than a square foot of canvas? Did you see the size of Reginald's canvas?"

Eve nodded. "How could I miss it?" This was the first time Jill had talked about being more ambitious. A good sign, Eve thought. "Sure, the canvas was large but it did nothing for me. All that empty space. I didn't know what to look at. Maybe that was the whole point. Maybe I was supposed to gaze into empty space and ponder infinity." She shook her head. "That type of art isn't really for the masses. People like me need to know what they're looking at."

"It wasn't finished," Jill said. "And you do a good job of interpreting art. It's instinctive. You feel your way into it."

"I do that?"

"All the time. Give yourself some credit, Eve."

Eve sat down next to Jill and handed her a glass of wine. "What I want to know is how Reggie boy gets up there. I don't remember seeing any ladders. A canvas that size, you'd think he'd have some sort scaffolding in place. Now I'm thinking he probably uses a winch to get up to the top." She tilted her head and tried to form a picture of the artist dangling from the ceiling. Eve laughed.

"What's so funny?"

"I'm seeing Reggie in a new light. Humpty Dumpty. If he fell, he'd do more than crack his head open, he'd leave a hole the size of a crater on the floor."

"I didn't realize you had such a morbid sense of humor," Jill said.

"It comes and goes." Eve gazed out the French doors. "No stars tonight but plenty of clouds. I hope it doesn't rain. I think I need to start a strict walking regimen."

She studied her hands. After hauling that heavy piece of driftwood the other night, she'd expected to get blisters. Luckily they hadn't come through but her skin still looked chafed and felt tender to the touch.

"I can't imagine Reggie being a mentor to Brandon. He doesn't strike me as the caring type. And you'd have to be caring and passionate about sharing. You know, the way teachers are." Eve leaned back. "The more I think about it, the less I can picture Reggie in a nurturing way. Although, I don't have any trouble seeing him belittling Brandon's art." She cleared her throat, and tried to do an impersonation of Reginald Bryant Burns, "You call that a line, that's not a line, it's a girly squiggle."

"Yeah, I can't imagine him as a mentor either." Jill took a sip of her wine. "Thanks for organizing the studio visit today."

"You're welcome."

"It can't have been easy to swallow your pride."

"It wasn't so bad. On the other hand, if Reggie had been there..." She shrugged. "I doubt I would've been able to hold back a growl. The man has a serious personality disorder."

"I'm guessing he didn't know about us going there today. Brandon McKay took a big risk sneaking us in."

"Is that a dreamy expression I see in your eyes?"

Jill took a sip of her wine. "He's cute."

"Yes?"

"I like his hair."

"And?"

"I wouldn't mind seeing his work. I wonder if it looks like Reginald's. It can happen when you admire someone's work."

"Yours doesn't look anything like Reggie's art."

"It does a bit. There's that atmospheric thing I've got going. I don't want to think I'm copying him."

"Even if there's a slight resemblance, it's not copying. Everyone is influenced by someone or other. And even if your art bore more than a slight resemblance to Reggie's, it would still be yours. It's like your fingerprints. No one has the same set. Or... or your handwriting. It's all unique."

"That's just the sort of comment Mira would make," Jill said.

"You couldn't have paid me a better compliment." Eve's lips stretched into a wide smile. "I'm going to grab some cheese."

"Have you given any more thought to what you're going to do next?" Jill asked.

"Not much. I sort of gave up on the gallery idea. I

wouldn't last a day if I had to deal with temperamental artists like Reggie boy."

"Maybe you should try your hand at writing."

Eve laughed and came back with a platter of cheese. "First I'd have to become a reader. I've heard Mira say that in order to be a writer, you have to first be a reader. You also have to be passionate about it and I can't say I've ever woken up in the middle of the night to jot down an idea. Mira does that all the time."

Eve knew it would only be a matter of time before she found something she was passionate about, and that, she thought, was an essential ingredient... a necessary driving force for success.

"How do you feel about cats?" Jill asked.

"I've never given it any thought. I used to feed one that always seemed to be hanging around the alley behind the restaurant. And my neighbor back in New York has one. She's a retired photographer and takes Missy out for walks on a cat leash. I can't say that I ever gave it a scratch behind the ear. Why do you ask?"

"The island doesn't have a pet boarding house. People go on vacation and they have to take their pets to the mainland. I've done the occasional pet sitting, so the demand is there."

"I don't know. What if I get attached and can't let go?"

"It's business, not personal." Jill nibbled on a piece of cheese. "I don't know if you realize it, but I'm trying to find something for you to do right here on the island so you don't leave."

Eve lifted her glass in a salute. "I've put your name on the pros list." So far, she had Mira, Jill and Jack. Three excellent reasons for her to remain living on the island.

"I guess if you really want to stay, you'll find a strong enough inducement." Jill plumped up her cushion and sat back. "Did I thank you for organizing the studio visit today?"

"Yes, and I think you've had enough wine."

"It's strange, I thought Reginald's studio would feel more magical. But it looked like a larger version of mine. And it felt like mine."

"I didn't realize I was supposed to feel something when I walked into your studio," Eve said.

"Not necessarily, but surely you've felt the frustration lingering in the air?"

"No. You always look so calm when you paint."

"Yes, but inside, I'm agonizing over every brushstroke."

"That's because you're a perfectionist and you won't settle for less than the best."

"And that's usually when I start to doubt myself. So I take myself off for a walk."

Eve laughed. "It all makes sense now. I don't feel the frustration in your studio because you come here to unload it all."

"And to eat."

"I don't want to get back to cooking professionally, but I do still enjoy the process of preparing a meal and feeding people." Eve stretched her arms over her head and thought about her date with Jack. "I need some new clothes to wear. Something elegant. Jack's seen everything I own now."

"You think Jack is keeping a tally on what you wear?"

"He might be."

"Men don't think that way," Jill said.

Her ex had. Alex's clothes had taken up all her wardrobe space and they'd often squabbled about it.

"Accessorize," Jill suggested.

"I suppose I could do that, but I'm not really into dangly bits and pieces. They get in the way and I always have to adjust things."

"How does Jack feel about you not knowing if you're going to stay or go?"

"We haven't really talked about it." Should she be worried? Did he maybe like the fact she didn't plan on sticking around? She hadn't really given much thought to where their relationship stood or where they were headed. So far, that had been a major appeal. Taking one day at a time.

"How about opening up a cooking school?"

Eve frowned. "That came out of nowhere."

"I'm going to keep thinking about something worthwhile for you to do, until I come up with... something. Hey, we could have a brainstorming session. Right here, right now."

"We've nearly polished off this bottle of wine. Are you sure you're up to it?"

"Well, it's too late for me to go home and it's too early to turn in for the night."

"Your parents are still planning their trip?"

"Yeah. Maybe I should start thinking about getting my own place. Now there's another idea. There aren't any options for non-homeowners on the island. Hey, you could open up a bed and breakfast or an inn. You wouldn't have to do any of the cooking, you could hire someone."

They both slumped back on the couch and stared at the flames dancing in the fireplace. The night had been cool enough to light a fire. Eve had always enjoyed the coziness of a room warmed by a nice fire and had been looking forward to the weather cooling down.

The clock on the mantelpiece struck the hour, the sound a light tinkle.

Ten o'clock. Despite all the food they'd eaten and the bottle of wine they'd been sipping, she was nowhere near sleepy.

"An inn," Eve murmured. "You could work there too."

"Doing what?" Jill asked.

"Artist in residence. You could teach art classes."

"I'm not qualified to teach."

"You don't need a piece of paper to teach. Mostly, people just need encouragement. A fresh set of eyes. A new perspective. Hey, we could start an artists' colony on the island. Have special weekends for amateur artists to meet and share ideas and talk about whatever artists talk about. And... I could feed them."

The sound of heavy footfalls had both of them looking out the French doors.

"Did you hear that?" Jill asked.

Eve gave a brisk nod. "Someone's out there."

The steps got louder and suddenly stopped.

They both sat up, but neither one made a move to get up.

"Should we maybe take a peek to see who's out there?" Jill's voice was barely a whisper.

"I don't know."

"Really?"

"Why do you sound surprised?" Eve asked.

"The first time I met you, you'd chased after an intruder with a rolling pin."

"Maybe I've learned my lesson. In fact, I think we should call the police." She slid to the edge of the couch.

"Wait. I think I heard something."

"More reason to call the police—" The sound of more footsteps had Eve swinging around. Calling for quiet, she signaled toward the front of the house.

Careful not to make a sound, they edged their way along the hallway. Eve pressed her ear to the front door. Frowning, she looked at Jill.

"What?" Jill mouthed.

"Heavy breathing," Eve whispered.

"Do you think there's someone out there making out?"

"That's the first thought that came to your mind?"

Jill shrugged. "It's possible."

A thump against the front door had them both jumping back. It had sounded like someone leaning heavily against it.

Eve looked around the hallway for something to use as a weapon. She grabbed an umbrella and slashed the air with it as if testing it. With a nod, she stepped toward the door.

"Who's out there?" she called out.

Jill clamped her hands on her shoulder and tried to pull her back.

"I'm warning you, I'm armed," Eve said.

"It's me."

They both frowned.

"Me? Me who?"

"Brandon McKay. Open up."

Jill gave a vigorous shake of her head. "This is too weird. You're right. We should call the police."

"A man knocks on the door and you want me to call

the police? We can't do that now that we know who it is."

Jill grabbed her arm. "Eve. Think about it. Running. Footsteps. Heavy breathing. This is the moment when the entire audience in a movie theatre holds its breath and then yells don't do it."

Eve thought about it for a second. Before she could decide, they both looked up, their eyes wide, the sound of police sirens blaring in the night mingling with the sound of their thumping hearts.

"Please. Let me in."

Chapter Eight

EVE AND JILL stood in front of the fireplace looking at Brandon McKay who sat on the couch.

He wrung his hands together, and then clasped them until his knuckles showed white.

He'd been sitting there for half an hour, not saying anything. Just shaking his head.

He didn't look dangerous.

He looked desperate.

And desperate people... acted rashly.

Eve's gaze dropped to the wine glasses on the coffee table in front of him. They were within easy reach. She tensed and imagined Brandon being overcome by a sudden, irrational surge of anger and violence. He could smash one of the glasses and use it as a weapon.

"This is ridiculous," Eve said, "Brandon. Look at me."

He flicked his gaze up at her.

"You need to tell us what happened. It's only fair. We could have left you out there."

He gave a slow shake of his head.

His furtive glance toward the door suggested he might be reconsidering his options. Surely, he didn't think he would be better off out there...

So far, her questions hadn't been below the belt. She hadn't even been pushy. Eve rolled her sleeves up. Time to get serious.

"This was a mistake. I shouldn't be here," he finally said. "I haven't slept in days. Everything's a mess."

"What is?"

"Everything." He shot to his feet, and then sunk down on the couch again.

Raking his fingers through his hair, he laughed. Again, Eve worried about him turning suddenly violent.

"I knew something was wrong," he said, "But I turned a blind eye to it."

Eve met Jill's gaze. They both lifted their shoulders. Neither one could make sense of what he'd said.

"How about a drink?" She'd already offered him one, but Brandon had just given her a blank look as if she'd spoken in a foreign language. "Coffee. Or perhaps something stronger." Something to loosen his tongue, she thought. "There's some brandy I use for cakes."

He brushed his hand across the light bristle on his chin, his gaze fixed on the floor. "This is bad. Really bad. They're going to try and pin it on me. I just know it."

"What?" both Jill and Eve asked, their voices filled with exasperation.

He looked up, the shadows under his eyes doing little to detract from his good looks.

This is it, Eve thought and braced herself. Whatever he'd been holding back—

A determined knock on the door had Eve growling in frustration.

"I'm going to answer that and when I come back, you're going to tell us what happened," she said, her finger wagging her ultimatum.

"Eve." Jill stopped her. "It's ten thirty. Are you expecting someone?"

"No, but I wasn't expecting him, and he's here."

Eve turned the porch light on but that didn't help her identify the person standing outside.

"Can I help you?" she asked.

The man was about Brandon's age. He looked slightly out of breath.

He stepped forward. Eve now thought she recognized him, but couldn't quite place him.

"I'm... sort of lost."

"This is an island. You can't possibly get lost here."

He looked over his shoulder and then back at Eve. "I was looking for the main road. My... my car broke down."

He didn't sound at all sure. In fact, she had the feeling he'd plucked the excuse from thin air. And if his car had broken down, then why would he want to know which road to take? Eve curled her fingers around the doorknob, ready to slam the door shut.

"Do you have a cell phone?" she asked.

He nodded.

"Then you should be fine." Eve pointed in the direction heading toward town and closed the door.

Waiting a few seconds, she nudged the curtain aside and peered out the window. The man made his way back to the road and that's when she saw his car. It looked shiny. New.

New cars didn't break down.

She'd purchased her car ten years before and there were times when it didn't get a service in months, and it still ran without a glitch.

She was about to turn away when she saw someone jump out of the car. A woman with long, blonde hair.

That's when it clicked and she remembered where she'd seen the man before...

At the Mad Hatter's Tea Shop.

A small fist pounded on her door. She knew that with certainty because she was still peering out the window and could see the small blonde woman standing at her front door.

Eve plastered a smile in place. "Can I help you?" she asked nudging the door open a fraction.

"I'm looking for my friend. He might have come this way."

Eve heard the sound of scraping coming from the sitting room. Not a chair, she thought. Possibly the coffee table. Had Brandon tried to make a swift getaway?

"There was someone here a second ago. He was looking for the main road and he mentioned something about his car breaking down," Eve said testily.

The girl rolled her eyes.

"If he happens to come this way, could you tell him his friends are looking for him?"

"Him?"

"Brandon."

"I'll try to remember the same. And if I see him, I'll tell him you're looking for him. Although, it'll help if I know his friends' names."

The girl seemed to hesitate. "Mel."

"Just Mel?"

"He'll know who it is."

Eve closed the door and waited to hear the girl's steps retreating. Moments later, she saw the car drive off.

Back in the sitting room she was surprised to see Brandon still sitting there. Then again, Jill was holding a fire poker like a baseball bat.

"Did our friend here get violent?" Eve asked.

"No," Jill said. "But he seemed to want to leave out

the back door and I figured you wouldn't be happy if he did that without first telling us what's going on."

"I'm sure Brandon only meant to stretch his legs, after all, we wouldn't want to hold him here against his wishes. That could be interpreted as kidnapping." She gestured for Jill to put the poker down. "Brandon."

He looked up.

"We're running out of patience. If you want us to help you, you have to start talking to us."

"I didn't do it."

It?

Someone had done something. Brandon was pleading innocence. And that something had brought the police to the island. Again.

"Okay. That's a start," Eve said, "But you've already said that." Again, she exchanged a look with Jill. "Does the police have something to do with what you didn't do?"

"All this time... He was there..." He dug his fingers through his hair.

"Who?"

"Reg. Now he's gone. Mel told me to get donuts for him. But he was already gone."

A horde of scenarios stampeded through her mind. Reggie hanging up his brushes and calling it quits. Taking off and leaving Brandon to deal with his house guests. "Where did he go?"

Brandon frowned. "He's gone. Gone for good—"

At the sound of a car coming to a screeching halt, they all looked up. Brandon shot to his feet.

"I'll go see who it is," Jill said.

"Here, take this with you," Eve handed her the fire poker.

"You don't think that's a bit too much?"

"Better safe than sorry. In fact, I'm grabbing a poker myself." Eve shrugged and turned back to Brandon. "You sit down again. Now, who's Mel and why is she after you?"

Brandon gave a fierce shake of his head. "You should stay away from her. She's bad news. She told me to get donuts. But she already knew Reggie was gone."

Eve curved her eyebrow at him.

"She's Reggie's stepdaughter."

"And the guy with her?" Eve asked.

"That'll be Stevie. His stepson."

"They're brother and sister?"

Brandon shook his head. "Stevie's from his first marriage and Mel from Reggie's second marriage. You didn't tell them I was here, did you?"

She shook her head. "No, I didn't tell them, but there's still time, I can call them back. I'm sure that's them at the front door again. So start from the top, Brandon. I want to hear everything that happened since this afternoon when Jill and I went to the studio." Again, she thought of the police sirens they'd heard.

Brandon shrunk back on the couch, his eyes widening. "You... you brought those donuts over."

"Because you asked me to."

"Not those donuts. The first ones. You tried to poison him. You tried to kill him. It makes sense now. After that, everything changed. He'd had dark days before. But not like this. I left him alone. If I hadn't... The next day it was over. I thought he was just having one of his dark days—"

"He was depressed?"

"A dark day. The dark side of the moon. There but not there. He shuts everyone out and we all knew better than to go anywhere near him. He was there, but he wasn't. And you tried to kill him, that's probably why he went dark—"

"You're rambling." She jabbed the poker in his direction. "Why would I want to kill Reginald?"

"Everyone heard you. You wanted him dead." Brandon sounded hysterical now.

"Yes, all right, I wanted him dead," she baited him. Eve flung her hands out. "Brandon, I know food. If I wanted him dead, I would have done such a thorough job, he wouldn't have lived another day to badmouth my donuts."

"Maybe you just wanted him to get sick. Maybe it was just a warning."

"You know what? You're right. I'm armed and dangerous. I could tie you up and force feed you a dozen donuts laced with the most dangerous strain of bacteria, you'll be writhing in pain for days, begging for mercy." She leaned in and tried to look menacing. "So talk."

"Eve."

She waved a hand at Jill.

Brandon's eyes widened. "You did try to poison him."

"The man was an oaf. In fact, he was a prime candidate for death by donuts, but—"

"Eve," Jill snapped.

"What?" Eve snapped back and swung around. "Jack." She took a step toward him only to stop. Several other police officers stood behind him.

"Eve," Jack said, "Put the poker down. Nice and slow."

This didn't look good.

Eve sat in the front living room, her fingers digging into her thighs. When Jack walked in, she slid to the edge of the seat. A police officer stood by the door.

"What's going on? Why am I sitting here?" Jack had brought her here that first night they'd met... when the body had been found in her house. She'd been a prime suspect then...

No, this didn't look good.

"You know I didn't mean any of that." She tried to smile. After all, if you smiled, the whole world smiled with you.

Jack's expression didn't waver.

He looked stern.

"Even if my donuts were responsible for making Reggie sick, it had nothing to do with me," she said imagining Reggie suffering from another bout of the runs, "Those donuts were perfectly good when they left my house. Anyone could have done something to them. It only takes some unhygienic mishandling—"

"Eve," Jack said in his best warning tone. She'd heard it often enough to recognize it. "This is Detective Mason Lars."

"Hello, detective," she chirped.

She tried to interpret Jack's lifted eyebrow.

This wasn't a social call and she should try to behave accordingly. Eve searched his eyes for the usual spark that meant he was doing his duty. Questions had to be asked, but he knew she was innocent. The spark in his eyes wasn't there.

The detective took the chair opposite Eve.

Jack remained standing.

A quiver of apprehension ran up and down her back.

Eve brushed her hands along her thighs and winced.

"Could you tell us where you were this afternoon?" the detective asked.

Eve did a mental rehashing of the day's events, gave

a small nod and replayed the day from the moment she'd woken up with a hangover.

She had nothing to hide.

Then she remembered the donuts she'd taken over to the studio that afternoon. "Did the donuts make him sick again?"

"When was the last time you saw Reginald Bryant Burns?"

She had to think about that. "I had dinner with Abby Larkin at Shelby's Table. Reggie put the spotlight on me. He told everyone about our run-in at the bakery."

"What did he say?"

Eve looked up at Jack. He gave her a small nod.

"What didn't he say? The man laughed at my expense..." She told them about the unfortunate encounter, right down to the last bag of chocolate chip cookies that had fallen on her face.

"How did that make you feel?" the detective asked.

"Not good."

"You must have been angry with him," he said.

"I'd been polite and he had nothing but horrible things to say."

"It incensed you."

"He didn't have to be so nasty. Specially not in front of Jill."

"Jill?"

"My friend. Jill Saunders. She's an artist. I wanted to get an invitation for her to see his studio."

"And when that failed, what did you do?"

"I took him a basket of donuts."

"These are the donuts that gave him the runs," the detective said.

"He didn't get the runs from my donuts. You can't prove that. The man has a voracious appetite for them. For all I know, he ate my donuts and the ones he got from the bakery."

"That would have been convenient. Tell us about the other basket of donuts you took for him today."

"There was nothing wrong with those."

"Are you saying there was something wrong with the first lot of donuts?"

"No." She speared her gaze at Jack. He stared back without blinking.

"I don't know what this is about. Brandon organized for us to visit the studio—"

"When did you arrange that?" the detective asked.

"Early today. We had to be careful to organize it by stealth because—"

"By stealth?"

"Reggie and his entourage had been banned from the bakery," Eve explained, "I had to be careful not to let on the donuts were for him."

"So you got them from the bakery."

"Yes."

"And then you put them in a basket. Why did you do that?"

"Because... because I'd promised to bake them, but I didn't."

"So you took the purchased donuts from the store bag and put them in a basket."

"Yes."

"And did you do something to the donuts?"

"No... Well, yes. I gave them a light dusting—"

Jack folded his arms across his chest.

"A dusting of what?"

"Sugar. I wanted them to look fresh."

"What were you trying to hide?"

"Nothing. I wanted to cover my tracks—"

"Your tracks?"

She gestured with her hands. "I didn't want Brandon to know they were from the bakery because I'd promised to bake them."

The detective didn't say anything as he looked at her hands.

"Ms. Lloyd."

Eve swallowed. "Yes?"

"How did you get those marks on your hands?"

She looked down at the palms of her hands and took another deep swallow. "I... I found a log I liked and hauled it back to the house. It was heavy."

"How heavy."

She wanted to be accurate. "Probably as heavy as Reginald. I had to make sure I could bring it all the way back to the house so I tied a rope around it."

"You had to make sure? Was it like a practice run for you to see if you could pull that much weight?"

"What?"

The detective gestured to the police officer standing guard by the door. Moments later, a camera was produced.

"What are you doing?" Eve asked.

"We need to be thorough, Ms. Lloyd. Would you mind stretching your hands out, palms up? Your co-operation will be much appreciated. It will help our investigation."

She looked at Jack but he'd turned away to exchange a few words with the officer.

"For what purpose?" Eve asked.

"We need all the information we can get to help us establish the time of death."

"Death? Whose death?"

"Reginald Bryant Burns' death."

Chapter Nine

"THIS IS A NIGHTMARE. Please tell me I'm still asleep."

"Here, drink up." Jill pressed a mug of coffee into her hands. "It'll do you good."

Eve dug her fingers through her hair. "They questioned me. Can you believe that?"

Jill lifted her shoulder in an easy shrug. "They questioned me too."

Pressing the mug against her lips, Eve took a long sip. "He's dead."

"Yes," Jill said, "Here, have some donuts."

"Are you kidding?"

"What, they're fresh. I got them at the bakery. It's doing a roaring trade this morning. The place is buzzing. Everyone knows about... you know."

"What?"

"You, trying to poison Reginald."

"Cut it out, Jill."

"I wonder if all this is going to influence my art. Picasso went through the rose period and the blue period. Imagine if I start a dark period. In fact, I might do that. Then years from now, I can point to the paintings and say, those are from my dark period."

"Are you done?"

Jill nodded and bit into a donut.

"What happened to Brandon?"

"The police took him away last night," Jill said, "But I saw him this morning. He went into town to grab a coffee. He walked right past me. I don't think he recognized me."

"So he's free."

"Why wouldn't he be?"

Because he'd be an obvious suspect. Working closely with Reggie. Running... from something. Running scared.

"Did you hear anything about how... you know... how Reggie was found?" Eve asked.

"There's a lot of speculation, but no facts."

"All that time Brandon sat here, he could've given us the facts." Eve gulped down her coffee. "Did he find Reggie? Did he call the police? And why did Mel and Stevie come looking for him?" She set her mug down. "I'm grabbing a shower and then we'll go."

"We can't leave the island."

"I didn't say anything about leaving the island."

Half an hour later, Jill grabbed Eve's arm and pulled her back. "You didn't say anything about going to the lighthouse."

Eve managed to drag Jill right up to the clearing where the path opened up to the grounds surrounding the lighthouse.

"I don't see any squad cars." In fact, there weren't any cars. "Come on, maybe we can see something through the windows."

"What if someone sees us?" Jill asked. "They'll think you've returned to the scene of the crime. I don't care to be your accomplice. What if I don't get painting privileges in prison?"

"Come on," Eve said, "If anyone stops us, we're out for an innocent walk."

"If you'd told me that before, we could have brought Mischief and Mr. Magoo. That way we could have looked more convincing."

"Where do you suppose everyone is?" Eve asked. "If we were asked to stay on the island, surely Reggie's guests were issued similar instructions."

They reached the front door. Eve tried the door handle. Locked.

"You didn't seriously expect it to be open," Jill said on a gurgle of laughter.

"This is a serious matter. A man is dead." And yet she couldn't bring herself to feel sorry for him. "I wonder if anyone will have a kind word to say about him? I'd hate to reach the end of my days and not have anyone entertain a single warm thought about me."

"Where do you think they'll hold the funeral?" Jill asked, "The entire artistic community might come out. I wonder if anyone will come to my funeral? I know plenty of people who'll send fruit baskets. A few might attend the wake. It would make sense for them to also go to the funeral before the wake. Then again, not everyone has a stomach for it. Do you think it'll bump up the importance of my art? Hey, there's an idea. I could become famous posthumously. That painting you bought from me could be worth quite a bit after I'm gone."

"I think that last cup of coffee you drank is kicking in." Eve pressed her finger to her lips and pointed to the window. "Crime scene tape," she whispered. Pressing her nose to the glass she could see the studio. The tape sealed off the door leading off to the side. She stepped back and looked up at the building. "The lighthouse," she murmured.

"What about it?"

"That's where they found him."

"Who found him?"

"I was just wondering that myself." Had Brandon been the one to find the body? Or had it been Mel and her stepbrother? And why had Brandon fled the scene?

They're going to pin this on me.

That's what Brandon had said. Several scenarios ran through Eve's mind.

She saw Brandon stumbling upon the body, then turning and finding Mel and Stevie who'd just come in...

Or, Brandon could have gone into the lighthouse and found Mel and Stevie and, instead of waiting around to listen to their explanation, Brandon had fled...

He'd been afraid of something... someone.

"Mel. My guess is she found the body." But she hadn't looked distraught. In fact, she'd looked cool, calm and thoroughly collected. A woman on a mission. And she'd been on the hunt, looking for Brandon. Because she wanted to make sure they got their stories straight?

Yes.

Eve would bet anything Mel had her stepbrother, Stevie, under her control, but she needed to bring Brandon to heel.

They heard cars approaching.

Eve signaled for Jill to follow her.

"We shouldn't be here," Jill whispered.

Eve peered around the corner and saw Jack and Detective Mason Lars heading toward the front door with another officer following behind, a camera in his hands.

"We'll go around the building. It'll lead us back to the road," Eve whispered. As they trudged their way around the building, they made sure to duck under the windows. Once on the road, they walked at a steady pace, until they came to the squad car.

Eve looked inside. "There's a laptop. Do you think they've got the crime scene photos stored in there?"

Jill gave her a tug. "We'll never know because we're going to keep walking."

The laptop was switched on.

"Keep an eye out. Tell me if anyone comes. And don't run away, it'll only make you look guilty. Remember, we're out for a stroll."

Eve tested the car door and smiled as it opened.

Crouching down, she pulled down her sleeve to use as a glove and slid the laptop toward her.

Eve grumbled. "Nothing."

"Good. Now let's go."

Easing out of the car, she saw a large manila folder in the back seat.

"Hang on."

"Eve," Jill warned.

Eve squeezed in between the front seats and again pulled down her sleeve to use as a glove.

She gasped. "Holy cow. I was kidding when I said he deserved a death by donut." Her eyes widened. A part of her wanted to scramble to safety and to wash her eyes with salty water so they'd sting so hard she wouldn't think about what she'd seen.

Yet, she kept looking.

Reggie's lifeless body... hanging.

She tilted her head.

He'd been hung with...

"A life buoy around his neck." If it could be called a neck. It looked massive and bright red. She nudged the top photo and peered at the next one.

"Oh, I thought that was bad. This is ten times worse."

The next photo had been taken from a distance.

From the bottom of the stairs looking up to the lighthouse.

Eve gasped.

She scrambled out of the car, grabbed hold of Jill's arm and pulled her, walking as fast as her feet could move.

"What... what did you see?" Jill asked.

She couldn't talk. She pointed to a path that led off the road and along one of the many walking trails running along the shore.

After five minutes of hurried walking, she stopped.

Her breath came hard and fast.

She looked around them to make sure there wasn't anyone hovering around.

"He's dead."

Jill gave a vigorous nod. "Yes. We know that."

"I mean, he's really... really dead."

"You look pale. What did you see?" Jill asked.

Eve pushed out a quivery breath and pointed to her

neck. "It was horrible." She kept pointing to her neck. "He looked bloated and... and he had a life buoy around his neck, and... Oh, Jill."

"What?"

"Remember the other night, we had the chicken and all that wine and then we saw that shape reflected against the clouds and we..." she pressed her hand to her mouth, "We joked about it being a donut."

"Yes? And..."

"It was Reggie. Hanging by the rafter."

"But that was... days ago."

Eve bit her lip and gave a quick nod. "Think about it. Yesterday... when we were there... he was there, but he wasn't." She raked her fingers through her hair and then flung her arms out. "He was there, but he wasn't."

"Slow down and calm down, you're sounding like Brandon."

Eve grabbed hold of Jill's shoulders and shook her. "Don't you get it? Reggie. All that time, he was there, but he wasn't. I hope I didn't say anything disrespectful. One shouldn't speak ill of the dead even if they were dreadful. And let's face it, he was horrible."

"Do I need to slap you?"

"No. No, I'm fine. Or at least, I will be once I get that image out of my mind. Oh, my God. This is going to give me nightmares."

"Get a hold of yourself, you're supposed to be the steady one of the two of us."

"It's easy for you to say, you didn't see those photos."

"Well, I hope you've learned your lesson. Never go snooping around where you shouldn't."

Eve drew in a deep breath. "Okay. I'm calm." She brushed her hand across her face and then stopped.

"What?"

"My hands."

"What about them?"

It made sense now. She looked down at her hands. "They took photos of them." She looked up at Jill, her eyes wide. "They think I killed Reggie. They think I hauled his body up there, and that's how I got the red marks on my hands. I probably used some sort of winch to do it."

"You did?"

"No. No. I'm saying that's probably what the police think I did."

"You probably shouldn't mention that to them. Especially not to Jack. Remember, you have to avoid pillow talk with him."

Eve just stood there, shaking her head.

"Are you all right?" Jill asked. "You normally have a come-back line."

"Those photos really shook me up."

Eve looked down at her hands. It didn't mean anything. The police would know she didn't have the upper body strength to pull such a heavy load. And Jack would have said something by now...

"Eve, your phone's ringing."

"What?"

"Your cell phone. It's ringing. Answer it."

She dug inside her back pocket and checked the caller ID.

"It's Jack. What do I do?"

"I've never seen you like this. What's wrong with you?"

"What do you expect, the police took photos of my hands." What did it mean? They couldn't possibly think she'd killed Reggie...

"Answer the phone, Eve. And try to sound normal."

Normal? She couldn't remember what that felt like. Normal was getting up in the morning and making coffee and thinking about what she'd like to eat. "Hello? Hi. Jack, hello. Yes, hi. Jack, how are you?"

Jill shook her head.

"Where am I?" Eve looked around her. "I'm... I'm home. Where else would I be?"

Jill slapped her hand against her forehead and shook her head again.

"Yes, I'm sure I'm home. You what?" He's coming, she mouthed.

Jill grabbed hold of her arm and started pulling her along the path.

"What am I doing? I'm... I'm running up the stairs... I left the tap running in the bathroom."

Jill gave her another tug.

"Why? Because I was washing my hands and then... the phone rang... and I had to look for it and I forgot I'd been washing my hands and the phone... it was downstairs. Yes, I'm upstairs now. Where are you?"

She picked up her pace and gestured to Jill to keep up.

"You're driving to the house. Okay, I guess... I'll see you soon." She gulped in a big breath. "Jill? Yes, she's here with me. Okay. I'll see you." She disconnected the call. "Keep up, Jill. He's coming. Jack and Detective Mason Lars. They're both on their way to the house. They have some questions for us. For you. And me."

"I gathered as much. What made you lie to him? You know it's only going to make matters worse."

"That's what I'm trying to avoid. If he knew we went snooping around—"

"We? No. No. No we. Please don't include me in your shenanigans. I had no idea where you were taking me."

They burst out of the path and into Mira's yard, both craning their necks looking for Jack's car.

"I don't think he's here yet."

Inside, they tugged and pulled at each other's jackets.

"Shoes. Shoes off." Eve pointed at the couch. "You sit there and look innocent."

"I can do that," Jill nodded, "What are you going to do?"

"I'm going to run up the stairs. Jack will expect me to be out of breath."

"Still?"

A tap on the window had them both freezing on the spot.

"I don't think he trusts you. He came in the back way."

Jack strode in, his gaze skating around the sitting room. Eve didn't know what to do with her hands.

"Jill, your parents said you'd be here. We need to have a word with you."

"Me?" Jill asked.

"Just a few more questions."

"Me?" Jill asked again.

Jack turned to Eve. "Perhaps you'd like to make us some coffee."

"Coffee? Sure. I can do that. Um. Would you like some donuts with your coffee?"

Chapter Ten

"I THINK they're trying to play us off each other," Jill whispered.

Eve looked over Jill's shoulder at Jack and Detective Mason Lars who were comparing notes in the next room.

"What makes you think so?" Eve asked and turned her attention back to the coffee she'd made.

"Jack didn't say much. He just listened. But the other one, Detective Mason Lars... he's a cool character. He shoots straight from the hip. He wanted to know everything, from the moment I set foot in the house to every time I saw you in the last few days. That set off alarm bells. And now... well, he didn't warn me to stay away from you. That's not a good sign."

"Actually, it is a good sign," Eve said, "It means he doesn't suspect us."

"No. I'm sure he wants us to fight. It'll be a battle of the fittest. If I think I'm a suspect, I'll turn on you. And if you think you're a suspect, you'll turn on me."

"Jill, I'd never do that. Relax. You have nothing to hide."

"No, I don't have anything to hide."

"And I do?"

Jill swung away from her and walked over to the window. "Well..."

"What?"

She turned to face her. "The other day when I came over for dinner, I had to wait for you because you weren't here. You said you had something to take care of."

"Yes? So?"

"Then you made chicken, but you know my favorite food is pizza and you said you couldn't make it because of your hands."

"I know. I showed you my hands. See, I have nothing to hide."

Jill looked down at the floor. "What did you have to take care of?"

"It was a figure of speech. I... I had all this stuff swimming around my head and I needed to walk it all off. Helena and Abby had left messages for me and when I spoke with them, they told me they'd both heard Reggie badmouthing my donuts. I was upset. You would have felt the same if he'd badmouthed your art."

"It was a long walk. You were quite late coming back," Jill said.

"I had a lot of angst to work through."

"Were you mad enough to..."

"To what?" Eve's voice hitched.

"Chefs can be temperamental."

"You think I killed Reggie because of what he said about my donuts?"

"The police are going to ask you about that, if they haven't done so already."

"What makes you so sure?" Eve bit the edge of her lip. "Did you tell them about me being late coming home that night?"

"Well... it sort of came out. I didn't mean to implicate you."

"Jill. How could you?"

"It shouldn't matter. You said you had nothing to hide. And I didn't straight out say you hadn't been here when I came to dinner. It was sort of implied between the lines, and that's why we have to watch out for that detective. He picked up on it. He knew there was something I wasn't saying."

"Is this what you meant by them playing us off against each other?"

"You're mad at me," Jill said.

"No. No, I'm not. I don't have anything to hide," Eve insisted.

"Eve."

They both turned.

Jack stood by the door and signaled for her to follow.

"We're ready for you now."

"I don't get this line of questioning," she said as she settled in the living room that had now been turned into an interrogation room.

"We're only trying to establish a timeline," Mason Lars said, his attention fixed on his notepad.

Eve didn't care for notepads.

"Now, if you can think back to the day at the bakery when you had your run-in with Reginald Bryant Burns."

Eve had to stifle a giggle; thoughts of lying down on a therapist's couch flooding her mind. She nodded. "What would you like to know?"

"You said his work was overrated and would probably only be worth anything if someone did the world a favor and snuffed him out. Is that correct?"

Everyone in the bakery had heard. "It sounds about right."

The detective held her gaze.

"Yes. Correct."

"What did you mean by that?"

"Reginald had been horrible and quite rude. It all just came out. I didn't even think about what I was saying."

"So the remark was impulsive."

She nodded.

"So it wasn't something you'd been thinking about for some time?"

She frowned. "No, I'd only just met him."

"You told a complete stranger the world would be better off without him—"

"Those were not my exact words."

"That's right, they weren't." He read from his notepad again and included some air quotes.

"You then went on to say, he was so full of himself he wouldn't need a life buoy to stay afloat."

"It just came out. Like a knee-jerk reaction because of his size and his temperament. You know... full of hot air. I know it wasn't politically correct, but I didn't stop to think. Remember, I was lying on the floor and I'd just been publicly humiliated. And... and he'd been mean to Jill."

The questioning continued for another half hour, by which time Eve had begun to fidget. "Would you like some coffee?" she offered.

"We'll be finished shortly."

She wondered what sort of measure of time he used.

Another half hour ticked by and she suspected she'd bitten her bottom lip raw.

"So after you had dinner with Jill Saunders, what did you do?" the detective asked.

"We sat and talked and... and we drank wine." She sat up and narrowed her gaze.

"Did you just think of something?" the detective asked.

Eve gave a small nod. "The night before I'd fallen asleep on the couch and when I went upstairs to bed, I saw the lighthouse light on."

"And that was unusual?"

"Yes. It hasn't worked in a long while." She frowned and tapped her chin. "When Jill came for dinner, we both saw the lighthouse light on again, except this time, we saw a shape. Like a donut."

All that time, Reggie had been hanging there?

"Have you determined how he got up there?" Eve asked, "They must have used a winch. I told Jill he probably had one to be able to work on such large canvases." Eve laughed because she again remembered thinking of Reggie as Humpty Dumpty. "Did the toxicology report show any signs of poisoning?"

The detective frowned.

"I'm assuming you had one done."

He didn't answer her. She remembered Jack had given her the same treatment when she'd asked him questions a couple of months before when she'd been under suspicion for another murder...

"You should be questioning his stepchildren," She continued, "Have you questioned his stepchildren?" She tried to think of the conversation she'd overheard, but her mind came up with a blank. Except... "They came looking for Brandon. Mel and Stevie." Eve looked at

Mason Lars and then at Jack. "I don't think Brandon had anything to do with Reggie's death. In fact, I'm sure he's the one who called you. He did, didn't he? He discovered the body. Although..."

"Yes?" Mason Lars asked.

"Nothing."

"Ms. Lloyd. If you have any suspicions, we'd like to hear them."

She shook her head. "Are we done here?"

"For the time being, yes. But we'd like to remind you again to stay on the island."

"Brandon had a smudge of paint on his face," Eve said as she hurried them along the path. She'd waited to make sure Jack and Detective Lars were headed toward town and had then suggested to Jill they go get her dogs and take them for a walk.

"Mischief, don't go too far," Jill called out. "Brandon's an artist. What's so unusual about him having paint on his face? I do it all the time."

"Brandon said he wasn't painting on the island. He's working on drawings, but not painting. So where did the paint come from?"

"He probably spends a lot of time in the studio. There are paint tubes all over the trestle tables."

"His jeans are smudged with paint," Eve said.

"So are mine."

"Yes, but yours look faded because the jeans have been through the wash several times. Whereas the paint on Brandon's jeans look fresh. You know, bright."

"What are you suggesting?"

"What if Brandon's been doing the painting for Reggie? Think about it. I overheard the gallery owner saying the last show had been abysmal and they could do with the publicity. I'm assuming the gallery is losing money from Reggie's exhibitions. That must mean his paintings are not up to scratch. Did Reggie have a show coming up?"

Jill nodded.

"What if he wasn't ready? Was he even painting? Was he painting anything worthwhile? You said there was something odd about the canvas."

"Slow down, will you?"

"Me or Mischief?"

"You. You're going off on a verbal rampage." Jill pushed out a breath. "But you're starting to make sense."

"I knew it."

"There was something odd about that canvas. It looked awkward. As if the artist hadn't been sure about the brushstrokes. It looked... it looked contrived. It lacked freshness. That spontaneous touch." Jill gave a firm nod. "Yeah, that's it. It didn't look spontaneous."

"We need to think about the reasons why Brandon

would be doing the painting instead of Reggie." Eve tapped her chin. "When Brandon discovered the body—"

"Did he?"

"I'm assuming he did. The detective wasn't very helpful."

Jill chuckled. "You need to hone your interrogation skills."

"When Brandon discovered the body," Eve continued, "Reggie had been... do I still have an embargo on any words related to—"

"Yes, but you've slipped up quite a few times, so I've already ordered my sable brushes."

Eve sighed. "Okay. Reggie had been gone for a couple of days. Did the kil—person who did away with him want him discovered straight away or did they want to buy more time? And why did they want more time?"

"Maybe there's a deadline for the show."

"And the pictures weren't ready?"

Jill nodded.

"So can we assume Brandon had been doing the painting?"

"I'm getting hungry," Jill said, "Can we head back now?"

"I don't have any food in the house. We'll have to drive to town and grab a bite at The Chin Wag Café. They've got the outdoor tables so Mischief and Mr. Magoo can come with us."

Along the way, Eve couldn't stop thinking about Brandon. He'd looked flustered the night he'd landed on her doorstep. What did he have to lose by Reggie's death? What did he have to gain? And who'd put him up to it?

"You're going to have dog hair in the back seats," Jill warned.

"That's okay. I don't mind."

As they approached the café, Eve slowed down. "Look, the wives are all there. Let's grab the table next to them. We might be able to hear something."

They made their way to the café, all the while scanning the main street to see if they could spot any of the other house guests.

Seeing a couple edging toward the table next to Reggie's ex-wives, Eve hurried Jill along. "Come on. We need to sit at that table." She dove for the chair and, looking up, she smiled at the couple and offered an apology. "Sorry, do you mind. It's the last outdoor table and we have the dogs with us."

Eve placed her chair so she'd have her back to the group while Jill sat facing them. "You be my eyes," Eve told Jill. "I'm going to try and listen to what they say."

Two of the women were dressed in black and they all had sunglasses on. Playing the mourning card to the hilt?

"I told Mel to be here in time for lunch," one of the women said. "Stevie's probably making them run late."

"Why do you always blame Stevie? Mel's the one who's never satisfied with what she's wearing. I swear, she goes through three wardrobe changes before she steps out of the house."

Eve waited for the third woman to pipe in with something. When she did, she instantly recognized the voice. It belonged to the gallery owner she'd heard talking that night at Shelby's Table.

"If you two had better control of your children, we wouldn't be in this mess."

Jill grabbed Eve's hand.

"The show must go on."

"How can you possibly think about that? Reggie is gone."

"And he would have wanted us to make the best of the situation. So what's the plan, Alexia?"

So, one of the two wives was as firm and determined as Mel. While the other one... was more sensitive, like Stevie.

"I've decided to do a memorial show."

Alexia, Eve decided, was the gallery owner and the main decision maker.

"I'll get my pictures out of storage," Mel's mother said.

"Me too."

"No. We'll go ahead with his most recent work. Buyers won't question the price tags because they know there will never be another Reginald Bryant Burns picture on the market."

"Except the ones we have in storage."

"We'll have to plan the release of those. All in good time. And we have plenty of that now."

Chapter Eleven

"MEL SAID she wasn't leaving empty-handed. Wake up, Jill. I remembered the conversation I overheard at The Mad Hatter's Tea Shop between Mel and her stepbrother, Stevie. Although, at the time I had no idea who they were."

Jill grumbled and burrowed deeper under the covers. "And you couldn't wait until morning to tell me?"

"It is morning," Eve said.

"Where's the sun?"

"It's coming. Come on. Get up. We have much work to do."

"Right, because something's afoot? I want breakfast in bed," Jill demanded.

"And I want..." Eve frowned. What did she want? She had her health. A few friends. Jill. Mira. Jack. Well, she hoped she still had Jack. "I want a new aim in life."

"I thought you'd already found one. Torturing me with sleep deprivation."

"You're young. You don't need sleep. At your age, I used to work double shifts and... Actually, I never really had much of a social life, but if I'd had one, I would have had the energy to party until all hours."

"Could have, should have. Would have. But you didn't."

"You should learn from my mistakes," Eve said, "No regrets. So get up. We need to do some Carpe Diem."

"Can I at least hope to get blueberry pancakes? And coffee, lots of it."

A short while later they were both seated at the kitchen table. Jill refused to talk until she'd eaten her way through one stack of pancakes. Eve used the time to catch up with her newspaper reading.

"We're missing an ex-wife. Two of them were at the café yesterday. But there's a third. And the men. We know Stevie was with Mel." Although, even after they'd finished their lunch the day before, they still hadn't turned up. They had, however, caught sight of Brandon going into Shelby's Table, presumably for lunch. Eve wondered if Brandon was deliberately steering clear of the group. Trying to distance himself from any sort of association with them because... he knew one of them had been up no good. "We should have been more thorough. There are eight men not accounted for. We can place Stevie and Brandon, but where were the others?"

"We're not traipsing through town looking for them because we don't even know what they look like," Jill said.

"Hang on. I think I've found something." Eve pointed at her laptop. "I've been scouring the online newspapers. The art critic wrote a piece."

"How do you know he's the art critic?"

"It's on the byline." Eve tapped the screen. "The last days with Reginald Bryant Burns. Not very original. I'm guessing he's going to write some sort of memoir or one of those unauthorized biographies that exposes all the unsavory details of a person's private life."

"Some art critics do that," Jill said around a mouthful of pancake. "They follow an artist around and then call themselves the expert on that artist."

"I suppose there's some money to be made on the talk show circuit."

"Are you suggesting that's a motive for, cue suspense music, murder?" Jill asked.

"I doubt the art critic would have gone to the trouble of... I'm running out of euphemisms here... do away with Reggie just for the sake of picking up a pay check." Eve narrowed her gaze. "Here's something. There's already a release date for a book which will include stacks of never before seen photographs." Eve cringed as her mind strayed to the photographs she'd seen of Reggie hanging from the lighthouse. "I wonder what Barnaby Reid will say."

"Who's he?"

"The art critic." She refilled her mug and stirred in some sugar. "And here's a stray thought. Will Reggie's tombstone be shaped like a donut?" She looked up and caught Jill staring at her. "What?"

"I didn't realize until now. You're a morning person. Talking a mile a minute."

Eve grinned. "For as long as I remember. I used to visit the markets before the crack of dawn to get the best produce for my restaurant. There was a lot of haggling involved."

"So what were you saying earlier about Mel?"

"Oh, you reminded me. Yes, the conversation I over-heard at The Mad Hatter's Tea Shop. Mel is after some-thing. She didn't want to leave the island empty-handed. She means business. I remember she gave Stevie a poke with her finger. Do you think she might be after the Picasso drawing? Reggie made a killing with the first one and rumors are usually based on some sort of fact. There must be another one, stashed away somewhere." She looked up and saw Jill grinning. "What?"

"You said killing. *Cha-ching*. This is all turning into quite a windfall for me."

"So how much do I owe you so far?"

"I'll give you an itemized invoice."

"I'm going to have to take your word for it. And,

we'll have to have a cut-off date. I can't honestly go through life excluding all those words."

"How about when the police solve the crime?"

"Agreed. Otherwise, you'll send me broke." Eve resumed her reading. "Huzzah. There's mention of the people present during his last days."

"Huzzah? I don't think I've ever heard anyone use that expression outside of a TV show."

"You have now." Eve scrolled down the page. "Pay attention. Robert Pierce, lawyer. Adam Cartwright, old school friend. Alex Green, drinking buddy. The others are collectors. This is interesting. There's no mention of Brandon. Why do you think that is?"

"Maybe they didn't want the name associated with Reggie," Jill suggested.

"Precisely. The more I think about it, the more convinced I am about him actually painting Reggie's pictures. He's like a ghost-writer. It's not something they... the person or persons involved in Reggie's... demise would want to have bandied about. They'd want to throw people off the scent. Imagine if word got out that Brandon was the one wielding the paintbrushes. It would devalue the pictures and throw suspicion over everything Reggie ever painted. This would cause a scandal in the art world."

Jill nodded. "You know, once upon a time, artists used to have apprentices who used to do most of the painting for them. I'm talking big names like Raphael.

They could get away with it because the job of an apprentice was to learn to imitate their master."

"Didn't you say you felt there was something not quite right with the painting?" Eve asked.

Jill nodded. "I guess Brandon is still trying to perfect the style. Like you said, everyone has their own set of fingerprints. That unique touch that sets them apart."

Eve drained her coffee and poured herself another one.

"Do you think Mel is involved?" Jill asked. "Remember Brandon appeared to be afraid of her. He said not to trust her."

"She comes across as a willful person," Eve agreed. "And now I'm thinking we're dealing with two parallels. The faking of Reggie's paintings and the Picasso drawing. And, somehow, Alexis, the gallery owner, is involved in all this. Remember what she said yesterday about Mel and Stevie being out of control."

If you two had better control of your children, we wouldn't be in this mess.

"Is this were you go off on a tangent and imagine the worst about her and everyone else involved?" Jill asked.

"I doubt I'll have any difficulty thinking the worst of that lot. Especially Mel. That girl is trouble. Brandon said so. As for the others... We all know lawyers are underhanded at best. If art critics are anything like restaurant critics, then Barnaby Reid has a godlike complex. One fell swoop of his pen can make or break a person's career." She tapped her chin and tried to imagine what would drive an art critic into committing... Eve slanted her gaze toward Jill.

Murder.

"Did you say something?" Jill asked.

"I'm thinking."

"As your friend, I feel it's my duty to now warn you to be careful. Don't start pointing fingers. There's a killer on the loose. Remember what happened last time."

She'd barely scraped through with her life.

If Jack hadn't come to her rescue...

Jack!

They had a date.

Eve threw her hands up in the air. "This had better not interfere with my love life. I haven't been alone with Jack in over two weeks. He's been that busy with paper-work. Now this... The timing is dreadful."

Her phone beeped a message.

"It's Jack."

"He must have picked up your desperate vibes," Jill said and poured herself another coffee.

Eve read the message. "He wanted to make sure I'm home. He's coming over."

Jill laughed. "He knows you so well. How nice of him to give you a warning."

"I'm going to change," Eve said.

"There's nothing wrong with what you're wearing."

"There's nothing right about it either. Scruffy jeans. I don't want to give him reasons to change his mind about me. We're still at the early stages. You know, dressing up for dates the way you wear your best clothes for an interview."

Half an hour later, she answered the door.

"Hello, Jack... or is it detective?" Was he here on business or pleasure?

Her shoulders dropped. He hadn't come alone.

Detective Mason Lars stood on her front veranda talking on the cell phone.

"Would you like a coffee while we wait?"

"That'd be great, thanks," Jack said.

He stepped inside only to then step back outside. "There's something different here. What am I missing?"

"Oh, you probably haven't noticed my new piece of driftwood. You know, the one I hauled over from the beach the other night." The one the detective suspected she'd used as a practice run for hanging Reggie from the rafter. How could he imagine she'd have the strength to shift such a massive weight? The thought alone was enough to make her arms ache.

One person couldn't do it.

It would take two, at least...

Mel and Stevie?

Mel, Stevie and Brandon?

Maybe Mel had tried to coerce Brandon into doing the dirty work for them, or at least, helping them.

She had the feeling Brandon would have backed away from anything that involved death.

He said he'd been working toward his first exhibition. Being mentored by Reggie probably entailed accepting other duties such as...

Fetching and carrying.

Procuring donuts.

But not helping to kill and hang Reggie...

"Eve?"

She snapped out of her reverie and looked at the display of paraphernalia on the veranda.

Eve frowned.

She went to stand at the furthest corner of the veranda as if trying to gain a clearer perspective.

"There's something missing," she said.

"What?" Jack came to stand next to her.

"Hang on. Give me a minute." She moved closer. "You know that memory game where you show someone a set of objects and then cover them and ask them to name the objects?"

He nodded.

"Close your eyes and see if you can picture what you've become accustomed to seeing here." He was a regular visitor. So he must have collected information, at least subliminally.

"The life buoy," they chorused.

It should have been hanging by the window.

"Please tell me it's not the one used to—" She clamped her hand over her mouth. The only reason she knew about the life buoy was because she'd seen photos of the crime scene. Photos that had been stored inside the squad car. Photos she should never have seen, unless they'd been shown to her. Or...

Unless she'd seen the body herself.

"Eve."

"Yes?"

"You were about to say something."

She rocked on the heels of her feet. Coy worked for some women. The cutie act did too. "Someone's stolen my life buoy. Vandals. Is nothing safe and sacred? I'm not pointing the finger at any of the locals. There are always so many people coming here for the weekend. They let their children run free with no adult supervision whatsoever..."

"Coffee." Jack guided her inside the house.

"Coffee. Yes. I can do that."

In the kitchen, she made more noise than necessary. Opening and closing cupboards. Setting mugs down on the counter. Jack's gaze never left her.

"Do you know what the penalty is for breaking into a squad car?" he eventually asked.

She swung around and gave him a brisk smile. Going by his stern expression, she realized her cutie act needed fine-tuning.

She was about to answer him, when another thought struck her. He hadn't placed her at the scene of the crime. The other detective would have jumped instantly to that conclusion, but not Jack.

Not her Jack.

He trusted her.

He believed her.

"Is it breaking and entry if the door is unlocked?" Eve asked.

He held her gaze in that steady way of his that actually spoke volumes. Eve smiled. While Jack's warnings came through loud and clear, she couldn't help feeling warm inside. Almost as if he'd drawn her against him and gathered her in his arms.

"I'm sorry, Jack. I put you in an awkward position." She wouldn't feel comfortable forcing him to choose sides. Jack had a job to do... and she couldn't stand in his way.

"And you won't do it again?" Jack asked.

"I don't know what possessed me."

"Neither do I."

They both knew she was skating around, and avoiding any firm promise to steer clear of trouble.

"Eve, I don't want you to feel I abandoned you. I hope you realize I had to pull some strings to remain involved in this case. I had no choice in the matter. I'm involved with you, so I had to hand the case over to Mason Lars."

Eve nodded. "I understand." In fact, the thought of being abandoned hadn't even crossed her mind. "So, about this life buoy..." He'd have to show her the photograph and even then, she couldn't be sure if she'd be able to identify it. "Just in case it is ours, I'm... we're not in any hurry to have it returned to us. In fact... you should go ahead and keep it... and then dispose of it." She had no desire whatsoever to live with the murder weapon.

She poured the coffee and handed it to him with a bright smile. "So, what did you want to see me about?"

He took a sip of his coffee, set his mug down and retrieved a piece of paper from his jacket pocket.

"Do you recognize this?"

"Sure, that's a copy of my invoice..." Eve swallowed.

"And this is the receipt for a deposit?"

She gave a small nod.

"A deposit for a painting by Reginald Bryant Burns made the day you visited his studio."

He'd joined two dots.

Eve tried to make the same connection.

"Um... I don't suppose your lab people have determined the time of death yet?"

"Oh, they have."

"And?" He had a reason for joining those dots. On any other day, there wouldn't be anything odd about someone purchasing a painting...

"I can actually tell you Reginald Bryant Burns had been dead the day you visited his studio. The same day you purchased one of his paintings."

"I hope you're not suggesting what I think you're suggesting."

The edge of Jack's lip lifted slightly.

"I want it on the record. I did not know Reggie was dead when I bought the picture."

Chapter Twelve

SHE WASN'T A SUSPECT. She wasn't. She couldn't be.

The life buoy... Used to kill Reggie.

The purchase of the painting... Purchased on the cusp. Too close for comfort and as bad as insider trading...

It meant nothing.

Detective Mason Lars cleared his throat. "The day you visited the studio, did you hear anything unusual?"

"Are the others being subjected to the same line of questioning?"

"We're being thorough, Ms. Lloyd."

Eve drew in a breath. So far, so good. They hadn't insisted she accompany them to the precinct. That would be bad. Very bad, in a formal sort of way. And there had been no more mention of her buying the picture with prior knowledge of Reggie's death.

She darted a glance Jack's way.

Eve had been doing that for the past half hour, using him as an anchor. The slightest nod from him was enough to keep her calm.

"Sorry, what was the question?"

"The day you visited the studio, did you hear anything unusual?" the detective repeated.

"Unusual?" She pressed her hands to her cheeks, her mind suddenly swamped with images of Reggie struggling. Had he been in the final clutches between life and death while she and Jill had been standing there in the studio?

"A bump. A thud. A cough. A murmur?" the detective explained.

She shook her head... several times. And just to be sure, she said, "No. No. No and what was the last one?"

"A murmur."

"No. If there had been any sort of noise, I'm sure we would have heard it. We weren't saying much. In fact, Jill was standing in front of the painting studying it in silence. I asked Brandon a few questions but only to buy Jill more time to study the picture. She'd been so eager to look at the studio and it had been so difficult to arrange, I wanted it to be worth her while."

"Did you notice anyone else in the house?" the detective asked.

"No. No one. I didn't even notice if there were any other cars. It was midday, so I assume the guests had gone to town for lunch. They don't strike me as the cooking type, and I'm sure if you ask around, you'll find they've been having lunch and dinner at various restaurants in town and never at home. In fact, I saw them at Shelby's Table and I know of a couple of people who saw them elsewhere." Feeling slightly more relaxed about the line of questioning Eve sat back and crossed her legs. "Now that I think about it, I didn't hear anything in the studio that day, but I smelled something. It was pungent. Jill said it was turpentine." Had the turpentine been used to mask the smell of...

Eve cringed.

If Reggie had been snuffed out that day or the day before, his body would have been decomposing.

Jack had said Reggie had been dead the day she'd visited the studio but had quite possibly been dead since the day before. He could have been hanging there for a couple of days. And that meant... Brandon would have been working away at the painting while Reggie hung around. Literally.

"Can you identify this?"

Eve leaned forward and, at the last second, tensed.

Detective Mason Lars had pulled out a photo.

She covered her eyes.

"I can't look at a photo of a body. Please don't make me."

"It's an object, Ms. Lloyd."

"Are you sure?"

"Positive."

She peered between her fingers. "I can't be one hundred per cent certain, but that looks like the life buoy that had been hanging on the wall outside. It has that sort of vintage look to it. But I'm guessing those things are all over the island." However, she'd bet anything hers was the only one that had gone missing.

"Detective Jack Bradford said you've only now realized your life buoy is missing from the front veranda."

"That's right. It was there the day my aunt left on her trip. I remember gazing at the display we have on the veranda and noticing it there."

"When Brandon McKay came to see you, was that his first visit to your house or had he been here before that night?"

"As far as I know, that was his first visit here." She shook her head. "I don't think he had anything to do with... what happened."

"What makes you so sure?"

"He's just that type."

"What type?"

"The type who runs from danger." She remembered how he'd recoiled from her when she'd held up the fire poker and when she'd leaned in and had wagged her finger at him. "He's an artist. The sensitive type." Her thoughts strayed to Mel. Eve didn't think the young woman would shrink back from anything...

Eve shook her head. "Brandon depended on Reggie.

That's my guess. He wouldn't hurt the hand that fed him. It can't be easy to make it in the art world. Just look at Reggie. He was surrounded by people of influence. Brandon would have benefited from that."

"That's very observant of you, Ms. Lloyd. What else have you observed?"

"I overheard a conversation between the wives and the art gallery owner." She figured the more information she gave the police, the sooner she'd be one hundred percent in the clear. And the sooner they found the... perpetrator... the sooner she could resume complete usage of her vocabulary.

Eve flung her hands out. "I can't believe someone used my life buoy to kill Reginald Bryant Burns."

Jill's laughter wafted all the way from the kitchen.

"Find the person who stole my life buoy and you'll find the killer. Do you realize what's happened here? Someone wanted to implicate me. I am being framed."

Detective Mason Lars exchanged a look with Jack. The sort of look that pleaded with him to take charge of his girlfriend.

"You've been very helpful today, Ms. Lloyd. Thank you."

Seeing the detective rise to his feet, Eve breathed a sigh of relief. She followed them to the front door.

Jack's hand slid to the small of her back. A feeling of excitement swelled inside her. He hadn't said anything about canceling their date...

"Are you an art collector, Ms. Lloyd?"

Her smile wavered. "No, I'm not."

"Are you an impulse buyer?"

"I can't say that I am."

"So you have a reason for buying a Reginald Bryan Burns painting when you did."

She looked over her shoulder. Jill had remained in the kitchen. She lowered her voice. "It's a gift for Jill Saunders."

"An expensive gift. I imagine it would be worth slightly more now," the detective said.

"I wouldn't know. As I said, it's a gift. Not an investment. That's not to say others wouldn't take advantage of the situation," she said. "Especially people in the know."

"The nerve of the k—" Eve growled. "The nerve of the evil perpetrator of this nefarious act."

Jill laughed. "If anything, this little exercise of omission is helping to keep your brain matter active."

"Can you believe they used Mira's life buoy? How am I ever going to explain it to her? She warned me to stay out of trouble."

"If they wanted to frame you, they didn't do a good job of it. No one in their right mind would think you'd use your own life buoy to kill Reginald."

"Why not? Two months ago I was suspected of using my own frying pan to... do away—" Eve huffed out a breath. "I've had enough. If the police haven't found a suspect yet—"

"What makes you think you're off the hook?"

Eve ignored her. "We'll have to do some digging of our own."

"Again with the we." Jill shook her head. "I knew there was a catch to you offering to buy me lunch. I suppose we're going to walk up and down the main street until we find the arty set."

"We have to position ourselves. Find a vantage point—"

They peered inside the bakery. "Do you actually believe one of them will confess to killing Reginald right in the middle of lunch?"

"You never know," Eve said, "They might consume one glass of wine too many and let something slip."

"And that's how you make yourself a target." Jill gave a slow shake of her head. "If the killer realizes you've heard them say something incriminating, they'll come after you. And once again, I'll be at risk too because, of course, I'm always hanging around with you."

"Don't be so paranoid."

"I guess there's no such thing as a free lunch," Jill said. "Except, that I'd hate to have to pay for it with my life."

"There. That's one of them heading into Shelby's Table. Good, I'm dying to try their dessert."

"Is it called Death By Snooping Around Where You Shouldn't?"

"This time, I'm going to sit facing them. I want to observe them. Detective Mason Lars said I have strong observation skills. He didn't use those exact words, but I'm sure that's what he meant to say."

They went inside Shelby's Table and waited to be seated. At a glance, Eve identified the art critic from his photo in the newspaper and Alexia, the gallery owner. There were four others at the table. Four men. During the following ten minutes, one of them had his drink topped up twice. Eve assumed he was Alex Green. Reggie's drinking buddy.

She drew a diagram of the sitting arrangement on a napkin and wrote the man's name next to a glass.

The man sitting next to him drew out his glasses and inspected a document. "I'm guessing that's the lawyer, Robert Pierce. They like to read the fine print."

"The detective was right. You do have strong observation skills. What would you say about me?"

"That you're exploitative and willing to make a quick buck from a person's weakness. And you're also a loyal friend."

Jill chuckled. "You're saying that because you don't want me to bail out on you."

Eve handed her the menu. "Here. Order the most

expensive dish on the menu. I'm having the Muddy Brownie Pudding with Honey Nougat ice-cream so if you choose another dessert, we can share and have a proper tasting."

"But what if mine ends up being tastier than yours?"

"Then... then I'll get you one to take away with you."

"So you're resorting to bribery."

"Just trying to divert your attention away from thoughts of bailing out on me. Now, pay attention and jot down anything pertinent to the case."

"If Jack heard you say that..."

"He won't. As far as he knows, I'm keeping my nose clean and out of trouble. I can't let anything ruin my date night. I need that date."

"At least you have someone. I'm thinking Abby is on the right track."

"You're not thinking of leaving too?" Eve asked.

"I might do the occasional weekend in the city."

"Then I'll have to come too." Eve took a sip of water. "I need to know what's in that document the lawyer is reading. I swear he's trying to read between the lines."

"If you were really serious about this, you'd engage the assistance of the waitress. Get her to cause a distraction while you grab the document, sneak it into the kitchen, have a quick read of it, or better still, use your camera to take photos of it, and then have the waitress create another diversion and return the document to the table."

"That's not so far-fetched. But it's too late now to go undercover." They placed their order and then spent the next few minutes trying to catch snippets of the conversation wafting from the next table.

The funeral arrangements had been made.

That meant the body had been released.

All the evidence had been gathered, and all the suspects continued to be confined to the island.

"We need to track their movements better. Tonight," she nodded. "They're all bound to go out for dinner. We'll park at the end of the street and when we see them all arrive, we'll head out to the lighthouse."

"You might have stood a chance of getting me to come with you if you'd been more cunning," Jill said, "Now I'm an accessory to a premeditated act, or at least, I would be if I went along with your half-cocked plan."

"How much do you want those sable brushes?" Eve asked.

"Not enough to get myself killed."

"I'd never put you in danger," Eve said. She recalled being chased by a killer and instead of taking the most sensible route to the beach, she'd headed in the opposite direction, away from Jill, because she hadn't wanted to put her in danger. "Everyone will be in town. The lighthouse will be empty. We'll have a quick look around. We might be lucky and find a door or a window open..."

"And what do you hope to find inside?"

"We won't know until we find it."

Never having belonged to the people who lunch set, Eve started to fidget. They'd been at Shelby's for over two hours and Reggie's house guests were only now starting to talk about ordering dessert.

Alex Green, the drinking buddy, had consumed two entire bottles of wine. The others had stuck to a moderate consumption, only drinking a couple of glasses each.

Their chatter had been entertaining, as each one had related some incident or other involving Reginald. He'd had a long history of thinking he could say and do as he pleased without repercussions. His friends had tolerated his behavior because... he'd been Reggie and had always known how to have a good time.

Success had come easily to him. His first wife had paved the way. She'd hailed from a wealthy and influential family. In no time, Reggie's art shows had become instant successes, with his paintings selling like hotcakes. But serious collectors hadn't taken notice until his third wife had come along; another socialite who'd dabbled in art by collecting it and occasionally painting a canvas or two.

"It's all about product placement," wife number three said.

Wealthy and smart, Eve thought. Having money didn't rule her out as a suspect. Some people professed you could never have too much money. However, Eve decided wife number three was too smart to become embroiled in something as unsavory as murder.

The conversation now veered toward plans for the future. Specifically, what to do with Reggie's estate. It surprised Eve to hear everyone expressing opinions. It seemed everyone had a stake in the estate, which included the massive warehouse space Reggie had used as a studio in the city.

How was that possible?

Were they all investors in Reggie Incorporated?

Eve watched the lawyer tap the document he'd been perusing.

"It's binding and will stand any challenge..."

That alone had been worth the long wait, Eve thought and stored the snippet away. It sounded like a piece of the puzzle that would come in handy at some point.

The conversation then veered toward holiday destinations and upcoming social events.

"We're not getting anything else out of them today. How about we go back to Mira's house and draw up a list of who's who with possible motives."

"What if Jack sees it?" Jill asked.

"We'll have to make sure he doesn't. As far as he knows, I'm keeping my nose clean. I can't do anything to jeopardize my date night."

As they made their way to the car, Eve made a point

of looking inside the bakery, the café, and The Galley Kitchen.

"Okay, everyone is accounted for." Meaning the way was clear for them to go to the lighthouse now.

"Do you want me to drive?" Jill offered.

"No, that's fine. I didn't drink anything at lunch." And Eve didn't think Jill would willingly drive to the lighthouse now.

"Oh, for heaven's sake," Jill said when she realized where they were headed.

"We can't let the opportunity slip through our fingers. It has to be now. They're all in town having lunch."

Chapter Thirteen

"YOU'RE MAKING PIZZA?"

"My hands feel better and I owe you."

Jill inspected the various toppings Eve had laid out on the kitchen counter. "Does that mean we get to kick back and relax tonight?"

"Yes, no need to go out." Besides, she didn't think they'd find anything at the lighthouse. They'd gone there straight after lunch and had found all the windows and doors locked. No surprise there.

"Why did you take a photo of the studio? We already have one."

"I didn't want to walk away empty-handed." The remark made her think about Mel. What was she after? She'd come to the island to be a part of Reggie's entourage for a reason. Whatever she needed to find had to mean a great deal to her. Or be of great value. Especially now that Reggie was gone.

"You saw something in the studio," Jill said.

"Probably. I don't know. What if I saw something but didn't notice it? There's a difference between looking and seeing. Now we have three photos, not just one." Eve punched down the pizza dough, spread it out and pricked it with a fork. "The newspaper article had a photo of the studio. I'm guessing it's current but predates our visit. You took some during our visit. So we're going to compare them all with the one I took today."

"Because..."

Eve shrugged. "There has to be something we missed. The day we went to the studio we didn't know we should have been looking for clues. Now we do."

"I don't think the house guests are losing sleep over all this. In fact, they're going about their day as if nothing had happened. They must be innocent."

"Or confident they can get away with whatever plan they've put in motion. I bet they have one. They all have an air of entitlement. And I don't think they're that happy about the way things are. Remember what Alexia, the gallery owner, said about the mothers not having their children, Mel and Stevie, under control. They're in a mess because of them. I want to know what Alexia was talking about. What sort of mess was she referring to?"

"Jack needs to know about that," Jill said.

"He's a great detective. He'll sniff his way to the truth."

"But, what about your input? It might help."

Eve shook her head. "I can't be seen to be interfering with the official investigation. Jack and I have an agreement. No snooping around."

"So what do you call this?"

"We're talking. He didn't say anything about talking."

Jill sighed. "All right. I just don't want to be in a position where I have to tell you I told you so."

Eve put the pizza in the oven and wiped her hands clean. "I wonder how Brandon is doing? It can't be easy for him, living under the same roof with people like Mel."

"Maybe he doesn't have a choice," Jill said.

"I think you're onto something. You said he walked right past you and didn't even recognize you. He must have a lot on his mind."

"Like staying alive and not having the murder pinned on him?"

Eve swung away and paced around the kitchen. "Alexia said Mel and Stevie had messed everything up. The night Brandon came here, they'd chased after him. Let's say they've been putting pressure on Brandon to reveal something? Or tell them what he's up to. If they've been pestering Brandon, then that might have put him on edge. Let's run with the idea that Brandon is faking Reggie's art. He'd have to focus. Athletes need to get in the zone to perform. If they're being badgered, they're thrown off their game." Eve stopped pacing. "Hypothetically, Mel wants the Picasso drawing and she'll stop at nothing to find it. Assuming Brandon has been working closely with Reggie, she thinks he's privy to inside information and knows where the drawing is."

"Big assumption."

"Brandon knows where it is," Eve continued, "And he refuses to tell them because..."

Jill clapped her hands. "Because it's a fake and he knows that because he faked it."

They fell silent.

"That's a possibility, but... if it's a fake and Brandon doesn't want the trail leading back to him, then he would have destroyed the evidence. Once he did, he'd have nothing else to worry about. So, it has to be something else." Eve checked the oven. "I'm going to set up the photos on the laptop."

"Can you print them?"

Eve nodded. "Great idea. Mira's quite the gadget girl. She has everything."

A half hour later, they were eating their pizza in silence, the three photos spread out in front of them.

"This is the best pizza I've ever had. I don't think I have room for dessert."

"Good. I didn't make anything special. There's only ice-cream."

"I'd never say no to ice-cream." Jill wiped her hands. "What's that?" she asked and pointed to one of the photos.

"What?"

"That cylinder."

"It looks like the sort of canister I use to store my pasta."

"Or something rolled up. A canvas. A piece of paper." Jill leaned forward. "It's sitting in the middle of the trestle table, but on this other photo, it's sitting on the edge of the table. That's the photo I took when we visited the studio. And... and it's not in the third photo."

The third photo. The one Eve had taken today.

"So sometime between our studio visit and today, someone removed it."

Had Brandon taken it the day he'd fled?

And if he had, where was it now?

And...

What was in it?

"Hang on. I'm seeing something else." Eve gasped. "Look at the canvas. It's changed from one photo to the next." She pointed at the last photo. "This is Reggie's painting, but in today's photo there are definite changes. In fact, there are slight differences in all of them. Do you realize what this means?" Eve flung her hands up and waved them like pom-poms. "Brandon has been ghost painting." She jumped to her feet and danced around the table.

Jill sat forward and studied the photos. "You're right. I think we need to confront him."

"Jill! I can't believe you said that." Eve hugged her.

"Hang around you long enough and your impetuous nature starts rubbing off." She shrugged. "I was bound to come around sooner or later."

"We'll have to corner him tomorrow morning. We're going to get answers from him, once and for all. All the pieces are starting to fall into place. If word gets out about Brandon doing the painting, the market value on Reggie's art will take a dive. The jig is up. I need this wrapped up by late afternoon."

"You're on a deadline?"

"It's date night. I told you, nothing can come between me and date night." Eve checked her watch. "Are you staying the night?"

"It's too late for me to go home."

"Are your parents still hassling you?" She watched Jill nod, but something told her Jill had other reasons for staying over. She must be worried about leaving her alone in the house. Eve hugged her again.

"What was that about?"

"You're giving up your painting time to be with me. Sorry, I short-changed you today. I left out the anchovy, it's never been my favorite pizza topping. I'm going to have to bake you a super large pizza with all your favorite toppings."

"I must have missed my rise and shine wake up call," Jill said as she strode into the kitchen the next day, her arms stretched out in front of her, her eyes half closed as she followed the sweet aroma of freshly baked muffins.

"I was about to give you a bugle call," Eve said.

"The muffins beat you to it. What flavor... no, don't tell me. Let me guess." Jill sniffed. "Blueberry."

"That's a given."

"Wait. Wait. There's something else. Chocolate."

"My back-up muffins."

Jill took a step back. "Why do you need back-up muffins?"

"What do you mean?"

"You didn't just bake muffins to please me." Jill wagged her finger. "I know you. Or at least, I think I've come to know you and your very peculiar ways. You're brewing something. You've been plotting. You want something."

"Coffee?" Eve asked.

"Don't change the subject."

"I'm not. Coffee and muffins go hand in hand."

Jill drew out a chair and sat down. "You're going to

make me guess or I'll find out what you're up to when it's too late and I'm right in the thick of it."

"Would I do that to you?"

"Yes. Without a second thought. You've changed your plans. Last night, you said you were going to corner Brandon."

Eve sat opposite her and smiled. "Okay. I've been thinking."

"Here comes trouble."

"Please don't jump to conclusions and hear me out. So far, we've been putting bits and pieces together from a distance. And we've done very well. I think it's time to up the ante. We need to get up close and personal. We need to infiltrate the group. One by one."

"Infiltrate?"

"Okay, that's too strong a word. I thought we might start by offering condolences. We've been quite remiss."

"Probably because you were suspected of killing Reginald. Going over to offer your condolences would have been in poor taste."

"I'll think of a reason. It'll be a simple matter of approaching—"

"I doubt they'll welcome you with open arms at the lighthouse."

"It doesn't necessarily have to involve a visit to the lighthouse. There should be ample opportunities for us to accidentally bump into someone and start a conversation in town."

"Right, because we all know how famous you are for starting conversations with people without incensing them."

"My run-in with Reggie was inevitable. He had a true artist's temperament and very poor people skills. Jill, we have to do this. Divide and conquer. We'll try and get to each one of the house guests individually..."

"I'm going to shut up now and focus on the lovely breakfast you prepared for me. That way I can't be held accountable for your actions or be accused of encouraging you."

"Here's my plan. We want to be thorough and talk with everyone, but we need to be smart about this and prioritize. We'll do that by using the information we have at hand. We know Mel is after something. We also know there is a canister, and we're assuming it contains something important. We can safely assume that's what Mel is after. The lawyer is also at the top of my list. Then the art critic. Followed by Reggie's drinking buddy. I realize we might not be able to approach them in that order, but we'll take what we can get."

Jill rolled her eyes.

"We have to start somewhere, Jill." Eve sat up straighter. "I suggest we confront Mel... in a nice way. We start up a conversation and let her know that we know she's looking for the canister. We'll have to feel our way through the rest. She could call our bluff or she could jump at the chance to hear we have to say, at which point, I'll... I'll make something up. It's all about setting the bait. What do you think of my plan?"

Jill snatched another muffin and sunk her teeth into it, chewing it slowly. "Isn't tonight date night?"

"Yes. But we're doing this during the day. We'll wrap it all up in time for me to come home and get ready for Jack." Eve took a sip of her coffee. "Actually, I'm feeling a bit guilty about tonight. You've been so good about staying with me all these days, I feel I'll be abandoning you."

"I do feel as though you're giving me the brush off. And of course, I'll be forced to go home and deal with my parents."

"You could stay here the night but—"

"Can I? Oh yes, please."

"You don't mind staying here alone?"

"We could swing by my place and get the boys. Mischief and Mr. Magoo can keep me company. They're great guard dogs and will let me know if anyone's lurking around the place."

"Are you sure?" Eve asked.

"It's either that or be ambushed by my parents who are now talking about driving all the way across to Seattle."

"I've been thinking. We could be mistaken for sisters,"

Eve said as they waited for their coffee at The Chin Wag Café. They both had brown hair and similar build. Eve had always wanted a sister...

"And your point is?"

"Just saying."

Jill covered her face with her hands. "Great. Just great. Now I risk being mistaken for you. I'll have to grow a set of eyes in the back of my head."

"What are you rambling on about?"

"Trouble keeps finding you and I seem to be making a habit of being near you when it does. Please don't go around cultivating enemies. I beg you. Otherwise I'm going to have to rethink our friendship."

"You're hardly my *doppelgänger*. But there are enough similarities... Hey, bingo. Here she comes."

Jill sat back and crossed her arms. "This is the part I've been waiting for. I've been wondering how you planned on engaging Mel in conversation."

"Easy." Eve stood up and put herself in Mel's path. "Hi, I'm Eve Lloyd. We met a few nights ago when you came looking for Brandon McKay." Eve didn't give the girl the chance to back away. She drew out a chair and said, "Join us."

The girl looked at Jill and then at Eve. "What's this about?"

Eve gestured for her to sit. "Mel, is it?"

"Yes." Mel sat down on the edge of the chair

suggesting the slightest provocation could send her running for her life.

"Did you ever find Brandon?"

Mel waited a few seconds and then gave a slight nod.

"Of course you did. After all, you're all staying at the lighthouse."

Mel's expression shifted from cautious to impatient. "What's this about?"

"I wondered if you'd found what you were looking for," Eve said. She hadn't stressed any of the words but she could tell Mel had picked up on her choice of words. Mel's face stiffened. "We know Brandon has what you want," Eve continued.

Mel tapped a finger on the edge of the table. "I see."

Eve wanted to clap her hands. She'd dangled the bait. Now she wanted more than a nibble...

"Or rather... Brandon had what you want." If Mel took the bait, she'd want to negotiate.

"And you know he no longer has it because..."

Eve did a silent happy dance. Mel had been after the canister and whatever it contained. It had to be the canister. "It's a long story." Eve knew dangling a tanta-lizing bait wouldn't be enough. She had to draw Mel out into the open, so to speak. Set a trap. Something to lure her...

"I have time."

Eve made a point of checking her watch. "I'm afraid

I don't." Nor did she have a long story to tell, certainly not one she could make up on the spot. "I can only say the canister is in safe hands."

This time, Mel put both her hands on the table. "What do you want?"

They'd hit the jackpot. Or as Jill would say, *cha-ching*.

Mel had been after the canister. And if Brandon still had it, Mel would have found it. How many hiding places could there possibly be at the lighthouse?

More than ever, Eve suspected Brandon had hidden the canister somewhere well away from the lighthouse.

Eve wondered if she could somehow wrangle more information out of Mel. Such as, the contents inside the canister...

As much as she wanted to get to the bottom of this, Eve knew she had to push the right buttons and force Mel into doing something desperate.

"I'm afraid we have to go now. Why don't we get together tomorrow and talk some more?" Eve suggested. When she'd said nothing could interfere with her date tonight, she'd been... deadly serious.

Chapter Fourteen

"YOU LOOK PLEASED WITH YOURSELF," Jill said as she settled Mischief and Mr. Magoo in the back seat of Eve's car. After their encounter with Mel, they'd driven out to Jill's house to collect her dogs and a change of clothes for her.

"I'm still doing a happy dance. Mel fell for my bait. I can really relax now and enjoy my date with Jack. I might even share our news with him, but I'll have to be careful how I phrase it. I don't want him to think we've been snooping around. Maybe I could drop a few hints and let him reach the same conclusions we did. I'm not after kudos. He can take all the glory."

"And here I was thinking you were competing for a place on the winner's podium."

"Who? Me? I don't have a competitive bone in my body. The only reason I got mixed up in this is because they dragged me into it by trying to frame me. Don't for a moment think I forgot about them using Mira's life buoy. Someone's going to pay for that." Eve looked over her shoulder. "Are the boys all secured?"

"Yes, tails wagging. Tongues lolling."

"I think I have enough time to cook something for you guys tonight." She drove off at a sedate pace, all the while thinking about Brandon and where he might have stashed the canister.

"Eve. Why are you tapping your fingers on the steering wheel?"

"Habit."

"The habit of trying to put two and two together? What are you thinking about?"

Eve pushed out a big breath. "Well, if you must know, I'm trying to figure out what Brandon did with that canister. I doubt he hid it somewhere between the lighthouse and Mira's place. Anyone could find it. People stray away from the path all the time and dogs like to sniff things out. Besides, Brandon had been frantic that night. I don't think he would have picked a spot off the path. What if he forgot where he put it?"

"Great. Now you've got me thinking about it." Jill nibbled the edge of her lip.

"Whatever comes to mind spit it out. No matter how far-fetched it might sound. We can toss it around and play with it. We could try to recreate that night. Maybe we missed something. We'd both been drinking. Let's focus. We heard someone running toward the house. Then they slowed down. And then they came to a full stop."

Jill leaned back and closed her eyes.

"Did I put you to sleep?"

"I'm trying to picture it all in my mind."

"Good thinking. Well?"

"Give me a minute." Jill drew in a big breath. "We heard the steps. Then nothing. I'm thinking he stopped at the foot of the stairs and looked around the veranda. Then we heard the heavy breathing. When you run, you rarely notice how hard you're breathing. It's only when you stop that your breathing becomes a little more labored because you're trying to catch your breath." Jill gave a firm nod. "So, while Brandon was trying to catch his breath, he..."

"He was looking for some place to hide the canister?"

"Yes."

"Under the veranda? Behind a bush? No, Mira's just had them trimmed."

"And that would be too risky. The canister is made of metal. It could glint in the daylight and give its hiding place away."

Eve pulled into the drive and, cutting the engine, sat back to look at the house. Behind her, Mischief and Mr. Magoo whimpered. "What are the chances the boys will sniff it out."

"It can't hurt to try."

She climbed out of the car and let them out. "Go boys. Fetch." They raced off toward the veranda as if trying to beat each other to the prize. Mr. Magoo, however, stopped midway and strayed off.

"I've been trying not to think about it, but someone snuck in here to get the life buoy. I hope they didn't come in the middle of the night while we were inside asleep."

They strode up the path, taking their time to look around. When they climbed up to the veranda, Mischief was curled up by the front door. "Well, so much for that. Although, we can't blame them. They had nothing to go on with." She sent her gaze skating around the collection of knick-knacks. "The rope is the only obvious place and big enough to hide something under."

"Or this piece of driftwood. Is this the one you brought back from the beach?"

"Yes. To think it nearly made me a prime suspect." She nudged the rope with her foot. The thick coils formed a mound big enough to possibly... maybe hide something. Narrowing her eyes, she bent down. "You're kidding."

"What?"

Eve gasped. "It's here." She dug behind the rope and retrieved the canister. Holding it, she jumped on the spot. "All this time, it's been here."

"Brandon must have thought it was safe enough to

leave it there. Otherwise, he would have come for it. Then again, they might be trailing his every move. He must have been worried someone would follow him so he decided to leave well enough alone."

"Until we put on our thinking caps." Eve grinned. "Come on. Let's go inside and see what all the fuss has been about." She waited for Mischief and Mr. Magoo to come but they seemed content to stay outdoors, so she left the front door open and followed Jill in, all the while smiling. "I think I might have to share this with Jack. We could say we were sitting out on the veranda and caught sight of it—"

"Eve."

Eve held the canister close to her ear and shook it. "I know, I know. Jack probably won't believe me. But you'll back me up. You only need to nod. That's not lying. After all, we were looking—"

"Eve."

"Honestly, Jill. You worry too much. We won't get into trouble. I promise."

"Eve," Jill shouted.

Eve stopped shaking the canister and looked up.

"We'll take that, thank you."

She looked at the men standing in front of her and tried to remember their names but her mind froze.

Her gaze dropped to the gun pointed at her.

A gun.

A gun?

"How did you get in?" she demanded.

A gun? Pointed at her?

Her heart pounded against her chest.

The man holding the gun chuckled.

Eve scraped her back teeth together. If they'd broken the back door lock or... or a window, she'd have a hell of a lot of explaining to do when Mira returned.

The man with the gun took a step toward her.

Eve clutched the canister against her and stepped back.

Robert.

Robert Pierce. The lawyer.

Of all people. And the other man...

The drinking buddy.

Adam... no, not Adam.

Alex Green.

Of the two, he looked apologetic. The lawyer, on the other hand, looked ready to pounce on her.

"Come on, hand it over."

"Why?"

"I'm holding a gun. I don't need to explain myself."

Without thinking of the consequences, Eve pulled on the lid and withdrew the contents.

It wasn't the Picasso drawing.

The lawyer shook his head. "You should not have done that."

Eve took another step back and unrolled the document.

A will.

Her gaze shot up.

The lawyer sighed. "This complicates everything."

So Mel had been in cahoots with the lawyer.

Yes, Mel had taken the bait. But Eve had expected her to come, if not alone then with Stevie in tow. Instead, Mel had gone running to her accomplice.

Accomplice? Or instigator.

Mastermind.

Ringleader.

Eve tried to catch Jill's attention, although she had no idea what she'd try to say to her.

Run for your life?

She waved the document. "You were after this, were you?"

The lawyer shrugged. "Having two wills messes everything up."

"Yes, I would imagine another will would rather spoil things for you." She tried to remember what she'd overheard the entourage talking about during their lunch at Shelby's Table. They'd all seemed quite happy. Robert Pierce had been going over a document with a fine tooth-comb. Had he been studying another will? He'd said something about it being watertight.

"This is a new will," Eve said.

"Smart girl. Too bad."

Too bad? She didn't like the sound of that.

"The police are on their way," Eve said.

"Sure they are."

"They'll be here any minute." And Jack would see her wearing an old sweater, instead of the sexy little dress she'd picked out for tonight. Eve gritted her teeth and growled softly. "You killed Reggie."

"I beg to differ. You tried to poison him," Robert Pierce said, "And when that failed—"

"How dare you. You used my aunt's life buoy as a murder weapon." Eve knew she had to keep them talking. Kill time so that Jack could come to her rescue.

Jack. Jack. Jack.

She filled her mind with his name thinking he might pick up the vibes of her desperate plea and come rushing to her rescue like a knight in shining armor. She knew it was all nonsense, but it didn't hurt to try.

Robert Pierce again gestured with his gun. "Hand it over."

Eve decided, right then and there, she'd get herself a Rottweiler. A fierce dog who'd leap to her rescue... or at least growl.

"And if I don't? What are you going to do? Shoot me?"

"Yes."

That wasn't the response she'd expected. Lawyers were meant to be smooth talkers and long-winded about it. They loved the sound of their own voices and... and Latin words... archaic words no one knew the meaning of.

He sighed. "I suppose you want me to bargain with you."

"I'm open to negotiation," Eve said, not for a moment believing he would be prepared to give her something in exchange for the document. This was far too valuable. He'd killed a man for it... Or had he? He might be holding the gun, but Eve didn't think he'd be the type to get his hands dirty.

Alex Green wasn't saying much.

Eve looked at him.

"How did you do it? How did you manage to get Reggie in the harness?" Belatedly, she wished she'd asked Jack a few leading questions. Reggie would not have been a willing participant in his own death. His neck had looked swollen and not necessarily from the rope that had been tied around it or the life buoy that had been a snug fit around his fat neck.

Eve tried to think what else might make someone swell up the way he had.

Food poisoning.

No, he'd already survived one bout proving he had the constitution of an ox.

An allergy to—

"Peanuts."

The lawyer grinned. "And you made it so easy for us by bringing him all those donuts he could never resist," Robert Pierce said. "Of course, at first we didn't know about his allergy so we tried other means. It's amazing what a bit of fecal matter can do to a person's digestive system. But Reggie had a strong constitution." He looked at Alex Green, "Then someone let the cat out of the bag."

His drinking buddy had stabbed him in the back.

"Of course, Reggie did play a part in it. After you approached him, he became rather obsessed with you. You gave him enough fodder to go on with for days. Putting the life buoy up in the lighthouse was his idea of fun. He wanted to see if he could send out a donut signal to you."

Eve couldn't help smiling. At least he'd managed to have fun in the end, albeit at her expense.

"He and Alex spent some time trying to fix the light in the lighthouse," the lawyer continued, "They set up the winch and harness. Reggie wanted to be the one to put the life buoy up there. Once he got the harness on, we took care of the rest giving him a donut laced with a sprinkle of peanuts."

She held up the document. "You ended a man's life for this?"

Robert Pierce shrugged. "We tried to reason with him."

Mel had said she wouldn't leave empty-handed. Had the task fallen on her to sweet-talk Reggie into giving up the new will?

Mel had messed everything up.

She'd been too pushy. Too impatient.

"What did he do? Leave you out of the new will?"

"He left us all out. After all the years we spent hovering around him, paying homage to him, listening to his incessant blabbering. He cut us all out of the will."

Eve couldn't help it. She had a quick look at the document, scanning it for a name. "Brandon McKay."

"As if we'd let the Johnny-come-lately walk away with the main prize. It seemed Reggie resented us. Said we always made him feel as though he owed us his success. All those years of us picking up the tab, of investing in him, and talking our friends into buying his art and he thought he didn't owe us."

Eve lifted her chin a notch. "You can't kill us."

"We can and we will."

"You'll never get away with it. They'll trace the gun back to you. You're already under suspicion. Why do you think you're still on the island? Jack's not going to stop until he finds the murderer."

"Well, he'll have a long search on his hands. This gun is not registered to me, or anyone from the group. Remember, I'm a lawyer. People in my profession meet the most resourceful felons."

"I'll... I'll come back and haunt you. You'll never get away with it."

Robert Pierce laughed. "Reggie was right about you. You're nuts."

Eve could feel her thighs quivering.

Her body had gone into fight or flight alert.

She knew she didn't stand a chance in hell of making a run for it. But she had to get Jill out of there. Somehow, she had to create a diversion and hope Jill took it as a prompt to run for her life.

She tried to fast forward to the moment just after she did something. Anything. She remembered seeing Jack a couple of months before bringing down the killer in two easy moves and thinking, she could've done that, if only she'd thought of it. She'd seen those moves in films often enough...

Think, damn it. Think.

In hindsight... what would she think she should have done... or could have done if she'd thought about it at the time?

Eve scooped in a breath, pushed it out and drew another one in. In and out. In and out. Until she could feel herself working up to... something. A furious rage?

Actually, she was starting to hyperventilate.

Think, damn it. Think.

Inspiration struck.

In an instant, she thrust her arms out, yelled at the top of her lungs and lunged for them, all the while telling Jill to, "Run. Run," at the top of her voice.

She was Mel Gibson in his Scottish kilt and war paint running like a madman in the movie Braveheart. She was a Viking gone berserk. She was a Banshee.

She succeeded in surprising them.

Robert Pierce and Alex Green cowered.

Before they realized she was all bluff, they'd both lost their footing and stumbled back.

Eve wasn't shutting up or easing back.

She screamed louder.

She grabbed at anything and everything she could get her hands on and threw it at them. A vase. A side table. Books.

She had no idea how she'd explain all the damage to Mira.

She'd promised she'd stay out of trouble.

And she had tried.

But trouble had found her.

That made her madder.

She kicked.

She screamed.

She scratched.

She remembered to kick in the right places.

She stomped.

She was fierce. She was possessed.

And furious.

This was supposed to be her date night.

She'd planned on soaking in the tub, relaxing and pampering herself for her date with Jack.

She screamed even louder.

Then...

The gun went off.

Chapter Fifteen

EVE'S EARS rang from the gunshot.

It took all her willpower to pull herself together and focus.

There'd been a gunshot.

Her eyes widened.

"You fired at me," she yelled.

The lawyer was writhing in agony. Clearly, one of her kicks had connected with a significant part of his body.

"You fired at me." She knew she'd raised her voice only because her throat ached. She must have lost part of her hearing.

Eve's hand shot up to her ear.

It was still in one piece. She looked over her shoulder.

"Oh, now I'm really mad." Her hands fisted. She turned back to the lawyer, pulled her fist back and aimed for his cheek. Her hand connected, slipped and hit his nose instead.

"There's a hole in the wall," she yelled, "How am I ever going to explain that to my aunt? I promised her, I promised her I'd stay out of trouble."

She couldn't stop pummeling him.

Not even when a strong pair of hands wrapped around her waist and pulled her back.

Her fisted hands kept punching the air.

"A hole in the wall. You shot at me. Now there's a hole in the wall. I'll kill you."

"Eve."

Jack.

She scooped in a big breath and let her arms drop. But then she saw Reggie's drinking buddy sit up. Eve launched into another punching bout.

"Eve. Settle down."

"What? I can't hear you." She punched out with both hands. "Let go of me. That one's going to get away."

"He's not going anywhere, Eve." Jack swung her away from the two men and carried her out of the house.

Eve couldn't stop punching the air, she was that furious.

Jack set her down on her feet and wound his arms

around her holding her for what felt like an eternity. Bliss, Eve thought and felt her body relax.

"Are you all right?" he eventually asked.

She nodded and gave him a small smile. She'd promised Jack she wouldn't get involved. Now he'd never trust her again. He might never want to see her again.

Then she remembered.

"It's date night, and look at me. I'm a mess."

"But you're in one piece. That's all that matters."

"He pointed a gun at me, Jack. Can you believe that? And now there's a hole in the wall. How am I ever going to explain that to Mira?" Another surge of anger had her propelling herself toward the house but Jack grabbed her and dragged her back out.

"Don't make me handcuff you, Eve."

"You wouldn't dare. They're the killers." She growled. "And that cost me another hundred dollars."

"What are you talking about?"

"You have no idea how much money I've lost these last few days. All because of them." Her breath eased down. She closed her eyes and tried to relax. "What are you doing here? It's not seven o'clock. You said you'd pick me up at seven."

"Jill called. We were over at the lighthouse. And just as well we were nearby. I don't want to think what you would have done to those men if we hadn't arrived in time. And I sure as hell don't want to think about what they could have done to you."

Her legs wobbled. "My hand hurts."

"You got him good. Where did you aim?"

"I didn't exactly have a plan of action but I didn't want to break my fingers so I aimed for a soft spot. He's flabby. I think I got his throat, and I might have hit his nose. I can't really remember, I was that angry. I could only think about getting Jill out of the house and away from danger." She fisted her hands again. "They had a gun, Jack. A real gun. With real bullets and now there's a hole in the wall."

He gathered her in his arms again.

"It was them, Jack. They killed Reggie. All because of the will."

"What will?"

"There's another will. It names Brandon McKay as the sole beneficiary." She rambled on, telling Jack about Brandon faking the paintings. Then Eve remembered what Robert Pierce had said about contaminating her donuts. "Jack. Throw the book at them. They used my donuts to kill him. He was allergic to peanuts. I don't use peanuts in my donuts so they put them in. Alex Green let on he was allergic to them. Did you know about his allergy?"

Jack nodded. "Did you say there's another will?"

"In the canister. Brandon fled with it that night he

came over here and hid it. That's proof of the motive. Jill and I knew we were on to something. Jill noticed the canister in the photos."

"Slow down. What photos?"

"The ones we took of the studio. We compared them."

"You did that after you promised me you'd keep your nose clean?"

"What did you expect me to do? They used Mira's life buoy. I suspected they'd used my donuts to make him sick. They dragged me into it, Jack. I couldn't stand by and let them get away with it."

Eve watched the police officers stream out of the house; both Robert Pierce and Alex Green had their hands cuffed behind their backs.

"I need some coffee." She stepped over the mess in the sitting room and put the kettle on. Sensing Jack, she turned to him. "You arrived just in the nick of time. Thank you, Jack."

"Is the coast clear?" Jill asked as she strode in with Mischief and Mr. Magoo.

Eve rushed toward her and threw her arms around her. "You ran. You ran."

"I had to. You were screaming at me to run. I'd been standing there, petrified. When you told me to run, I nearly collapsed. My legs started moving and they didn't stop until I reached the road. Then I realized I'd pulled my phone out and I'd dialed for help. They must have thought I was crazy the way I was raving and ranting."

"I'm so glad you ran. Thank you."

Moments later they were sipping their coffees.

Jack set his mug down. "Explain to me again how Robert Pierce and Alex Green knew about the canister being here?"

Oh, Eve realized she'd skipped over that part.

"I've got some muffins. Would you like some muffins?"

"No, thanks." Jack held her gaze.

"This coffee tastes so good. I thought I wouldn't live long enough to drink another cup."

"Eve."

"Yes?" She sighed. "All right. We—"

Jill cleared her throat.

"I knew they were after something. I'd overheard Mel say she wasn't leaving the island until she got what she came for. I just didn't know what that could be." She shrugged. "Then we... I noticed the canister in the photos. There was only one way to find out if the canister had any value. So I decided to set the bait and mention it to Mel. If she reacted in any way... if she showed any interest, then it meant she wanted whatever was inside the canister."

"Did you, at any point, consider passing that information on to the police?"

"Well, I couldn't."

"Why?"

"Because I'd promised to keep my nose clean."

"But you didn't."

"What was I supposed to do? The information landed on my lap. I thought Mel was after the Picasso drawing."

"What Picasso drawing?"

Eve told him about the article she'd read and how there was supposed to be another drawing floating around. "I assumed she was after the drawing. It never occurred to me to imagine there'd be a will tucked inside. Although, it makes sense now. Alexia, the gallery owner, said Mel and Stevie had messed everything up. I think she meant Mel had been badgering Reggie to come clean about the new will. But you're a great detective. I'm sure you'll get to the bottom of it."

"I'm glad to know you have some faith in my abilities."

Yet he didn't sound too pleased with her.

"I can't believe... Do you realize... Do you have any idea the danger you put yourselves in?" He brushed his hand across his face. "What exactly did you think Mel was going to do after you told her you had what she wanted?"

Eve shrugged. "I thought she'd take some time to cool off and then come to see me. I never expected her to tell Robert Pierce. You should dig into his activities. He said he got the gun from one of his criminal friends."

Jack stood up. "Thanks for the coffee. I should get going." He started to say something else, but then stopped. He stared at her for a moment.

Eve shifted. "I guess date night's off."

"Sorry. I'll make it up to you."

"I'm feeling deflated," Eve said, "It's the morning after syndrome. So much has happened, now I'm at a loss."

They'd cleaned up the house and had organized to have the hole in the wall fixed before Mira returned.

"Have you heard from Jack?" Jill asked.

"He called to ask how I was doing."

"And?"

"I tried pretending I wasn't interested in the case."

Jill laughed. "How long did that last?"

"I had to ask. It would have been rude not to. Besides, I need to show an interest in Jack's work, otherwise he'll think I'm losing interest in him. He said they've hauled all the house guests in for further questioning. Robert Pierce and Alex Green have been charged. Going by what Robert Pierce said, he and Alex Green were the only ones involved in actually... doing away... Hey, it's over. The crime's been solved. My embargo's lifted. They killed Reggie. They murdered him. And they used my donuts and Mira's life buoy to kill him."

Jill laughed. "I told you so. I knew you'd eventually explode."

"How would you like it if I banned you from saying I told you so."

Jill tilted her head. "You're right about that feeling of being at a loss. What are we going to do with ourselves? This has been quite an adrenaline rush."

"We'll go out for breakfast. My shout. And we need to go shopping for a life buoy. If Mira realizes it's missing, she'll know something happened."

They got as far as the car.

"Hey, there's Jack." Eve watched him climb out of his car and stride toward them.

She'd been trying to avoid thinking about the date they'd missed, but now that he'd come...

Had he forgiven her for breaking her promise?

"Hello, Jack. You nearly missed us. We were on our way into town for breakfast."

"Mind if I join you? I've been looking forward to a break."

Eve supposed that meant he didn't want to talk about work, or anything related to the case.

"Actually, you'll love this, Eve. Detective Mason Lars is impressed by you. He said you've missed your calling. He wants to know your secret."

Was that a hint of jealousy? "Common sense deductive thinking," Eve smiled, "What's Mel been charged with?"

"Nothing as yet," Jack said, "She's pleading innocent."

"What? No. She's guilty."

"Eve. We'll get to the bottom of this." He smiled. "You've done your part, now let the police do their job."

She told me to get donuts. But she already knew Reggie was gone.

"Are you telling me to keep right out of it?" Eve asked.

"For your own good," Jack said.

"So if I had an important piece of information—"

Jack shook his head. "All right. Out with it."

"I'll trade you."

Jack brushed his hand across his face.

"Who discovered the body?" Eve asked.

"Brandon McKay."

"I knew it," Eve said. "And he called the police."

Jack nodded.

"Well, the night Brandon ran to the beach house, he was raving. He said Mel had told him to get the donuts even though Reggie was already gone, although Brandon didn't know that at the time." Eve smiled at Jill. "They still wanted Brandon to keep faking the pictures. So they made him believe Reggie was still alive but keeping to himself. Mel's as guilty as the others. You only need to get Brandon McKay to collaborate and confirm this..."

Jill nudged her.

"What?"

"You can't tell Jack how to run his investigation."

"I'm only making suggestions. Besides, I have an adage to live up to."

"Behind every successful man is a woman?" Jill asked.

"Yes. Although, I don't want to assume. Especially since our date was postponed. For all I know it was actually canceled and Jack will never want anything more to do with me."

Jack brushed his hand across her back. Reaching inside his car, he brought out a bunch of flowers.

"He brought you flowers," Jill said. "That's a good sign. It has to be."

"I think I need to apply my deductive thinking. Do you think he's trying to make up for the date we missed? And was the date postponed or canceled? There is a difference."

"The flowers have to mean something," Jill agreed. "Maybe he felt he needed to apologize."

Jack cleared his throat.

"But it wasn't his fault. In fact, I should own up and accept some responsibility for ruining our date night. If I hadn't broken my promise to him and Mira—"

"Eve," Jack said.

"Hang on, Jack. Give us a minute. Jill and I will figure this out..."

Jack shook his head. "I suppose the sooner I get used to this, the better."

Eve smiled and thought she'd never been happier to see him.

Manufactured by Amazon.ca
Bolton, ON

15130288R00109